ZOOBREAK

ZOOBREAK

GORDON KORMAN

Scholastic Inc.
New York Toronto London Auckland
Sydney Mexico City New Delhi Hong Kong

This book was originally published in hardcover
by Scholastic Press in 2009.

ISBN 978-0-545-12500-0

12 11 10 9 8 7 6 5 4 3   10 11 12 13 14 15/0

Printed in the U.S.A.   40
First Scholastic paperback printing, February 2010

The text type was set in ITC Century.
Book design by Elizabeth B. Parisi

For Elizabeth Harding,
who steers the boat.

And special thanks to
Jennifer Hershey,
zookeeper to the stars.

1

THE PEOPLE

VS.

MR. DRYSDALE (PERSON)

AND CLEOPATRA DRYSDALE (MONKEY)

CLOSING ARGUMENT: Ladies and gentlemen of the jury, the DEFENSE has shown that when Officer McElroy gave Mr. Drysdale a TICKET for UNSAFE DRIVING, this was NOT FAIR because:

(i) Mr. Drysdale was not breaking any laws.

(ii) Luthor Drysdale (dog) was hanging his head out the window, which every dog does.

(iii) Everyone in Cedarville knows that Cleopatra always rides on the back of Luthor's neck, whether driving in a car or not.

Officer McElroy claims that Cleopatra could have fallen off, creating a TRAFFIC HAZARD. However, the defense has proven that capuchin monkeys are excellent GRIPPERS and have been hanging off of tree branches, dogs' necks, etc. for THOUSANDS of YEARS. We therefore ask you, ladies and gentlemen of the jury, to return a verdict of NOT GUILTY so Mr. Drysdale won't have to pay the fifty-dollar fine.

Ben Slovak looked up from the paper. "Do they have juries in traffic court?"

"Okay, I'll change it to 'Your Honor.'" Griffin Bing was impatient. "What about the reasoning? Perfect, right?"

Ben wanted to agree with Griffin. Life was so much smoother when you did.

"I guess so," he said uncertainly. "But wouldn't it be easier just to pay the ticket?"

"Never!" Griffin thundered. "There can't possibly be a law against driving around with a monkey piggybacking your dog! The whole thing comes down to that cop saying it isn't safe. Who do you think knows more about animals — the cop or Savannah?"

No contest there. Their fellow sixth grader Savannah Drysdale was Cedarville's greatest authority on animals. In addition to Cleopatra and Luthor, she was the housemate — she refused to call herself the owner — of cats, rabbits, hamsters, turtles, a parakeet, and an albino chameleon.

Ben looked distracted. "Listen, Griffin, I need to talk to you about something."

"Later," Griffin promised. "I want to get this over to Savannah's. I can't wait to see the look on her face when she reads our plan for her dad's defense."

Wordlessly, Ben followed Griffin down the street and up the Drysdales' front walk. You didn't argue with Griffin when there was a plan involved. In this town, Griffin Bing was The Man With The Plan.

Griffin marched up to the house and rang the bell. Almost instantly, the door was flung open and Savannah burst out onto the porch, eyes wild.

"You've got to help me!" she cried.

Griffin thrust the paper into her hand. "Don't worry, we have a plan."

Savannah stared at the closing argument like it was written in Martian. "What's this supposed to be?"

"Your father's defense for the traffic ticket!"

"Are you nuts?" Savannah wailed. "Nobody cares about the ticket! Cleopatra is *gone*!"

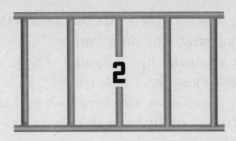

2

"Gone?" Griffin repeated. "Gone where?"

Savannah could barely contain herself. "Well, if I knew that, I'd go get her back, wouldn't I?"

"When did you last see her?" Ben asked with kind concern.

"She was puttering around the backyard, relaxing in the hammock and listening to NPR. And when I came out with her plantains, she wasn't there anymore!"

"You mean you left her outside all alone?" Griffin asked. "She probably ran away."

Savannah was indignant. "She's a monkey, not a wild animal! Cleo knows where she lives. Something's happened to her! She would never just leave like this." She wiped at her watery eyes. "Poor Luthor!"

Ben was mystified. "If Cleopatra is the one who's missing, why poor Luthor?"

She regarded him pityingly. "How would you like to lose *your* best friend?"

Ben assumed a stricken look and turned to Griffin. "I really need to talk to you about something, man!"

Before Griffin could respond, the door swung wide again, and out slunk Luthor.

Both boys froze, poised for flight. Savannah might have thought her dog was the mildest, sweetest creature on earth, but Griffin and Ben did not share her opinion. Luthor was a large brown and black Doberman with rippling muscles and jaws as wide as a small hippo's. Not long ago, this animal had been a trained guard dog, mean as they come. It had taken all Savannah's skills as a dog whisperer to bring him down to merely vicious.

But they could see right away that Luthor was not himself. His taut, athletic belly practically dragged on the floor, and his face sagged with sadness. From time to time, he would swipe at the back of his neck, as if feeling for the absent monkey. His constant threatening growl had been replaced by a sad whimpering sound.

"We've got posters all over town," Savannah went on. "I can't leave the house, in case somebody phones. You've got to do this for me!"

Griffin was cautious. "Do what?"

"I thought of a few extra places we forgot to search the first time around — places Cleo really likes. The jungle gym at Growing Minds Day Care; the blue box behind the Chinese restaurant where they throw out the empty pineapple tins; and the top of that shaky dryer at the Laundromat." She stopped for breath. "Take Luthor. He'll be able to pick up Cleo's scent."

She held out the big dog's leash. They made no move to take it.

Griffin gulped. "Are you sure this is a good idea?"

Savannah patted the dog sympathetically. "The poor, sweet baby needs to feel like he's helping. He's so upset he can't even eat."

"Can I get that in writing?" Ben asked nervously.

Dumpster-diving behind the Mandarin Palace was a smelly and sticky business. But Luthor had no interest in licking the sweet syrup from the pineapple tins. Nor did the Doberman pick up any trace of his lost monkey friend.

"This is perfect," Ben complained. "Hanging out in the garbage with a killing machine! Does he even know what he's supposed to be looking for?"

Griffin held on to the leash with both hands, as if landing a fighting marlin. "Savannah says when he picks up the scent, he'll practically go berserk."

"And that's a *good* thing?" Ben squeaked. "I like him this way — depressed, harmless. Let's run him by the day care and the Laundromat before he gets his appetite back!"

"You think I'm thrilled about this?" Griffin said irritably. "I'm the one holding the leash. Look, Savannah's our friend. You know how much animals mean to her."

Luthor drooped beside the Dumpster and emitted a yawn that opened his mouth wide enough to accommodate a good-sized head.

"What if the monkey just ran away?" Ben asked shakily.

"Of course it ran away," Griffin agreed. "But if Savannah needs to search every inch of Cedarville before she admits that, we have to let her. Come on, let's hit the day care before they empty out the Diaper Genie."

There was no sign of Cleopatra at Growing Minds. And at the Laundromat, two cats were established atop the shaky dryer. No monkey.

Ben sighed with relief. "Okay, now we take Luthor home, right?"

They were halfway back to the Drysdale house when a sudden bark erupted from the Doberman. The next second, the leash was wrenched from Griffin's hand as the big dog galloped across lawns and through flower beds.

"Savannah's going to kill us!" Ben panted as they pursued the runaway. "First the monkey, now Luthor!"

"We can't lose him!" gasped Griffin.

By the time they caught up with him, the Doberman was in such a state of excitement that they didn't dare go closer than twenty feet. The animal leaped about, springing on powerful legs, an urgent high-pitched whine issuing from deep in his throat.

Griffin pointed. "What's that in his mouth?"

Then the dog was off again, barreling down the street at breakneck speed. He vaulted over the gate at the Drysdale home and ran full tilt into the front door. The thud seemed to echo off every building in Cedarville.

Griffin and Ben bounded up the walk just as Savannah appeared on the porch. Luthor deposited an object on the mat at her feet.

It was a blackened, squashed, half-eaten banana.

"Oh, my God!" Savannah quavered. "Cleo's been kidnapped!"

Griffin was blown away. "It says that on the banana?"

"Don't you see? It was used to lure her out of our yard!"

Ben chose his words carefully. "Yeah, but how do you know that isn't just a regular banana somebody dropped?"

"Are you blind? Cleo's scent is all over it! Why do you think Luthor's acting this way?"

"He's hungry?" Ben suggested feebly.

Yet it was obvious that the Doberman was not eating his find. His intention had always been to bring it to Savannah.

She was devastated. "This is even worse than I thought! Cleo isn't lost! She's been abducted! I've got to update the police!" She wheeled and disappeared into the house, Luthor at her heels.

"You're welcome," Ben called after her.

Griffin turned to go. "Take it easy on Savannah. This is her worst nightmare come true. I even feel kind of bad for the mutt. Maybe he really is sad about losing his friend."

Ben blanched. "Griffin, I have to go to boarding school," he blurted.

"I mean, you wouldn't think a hungry beast could have feelings, but —" Griffin pulled up short. "What did you just say?"

Ben's expression was tragic. "There's this special boarding school for kids with sleep disorders. I'm number one on the waiting list for the next open spot." Ben suffered from narcolepsy, a condition which could make him fall asleep suddenly at any hour of the day or night.

Griffin was shocked. "But I thought that's all under control! That's why you take those special naps during the day."

"The academy has the top experts in the country," Ben explained. "They'll know things to try that a doctor in a little town on Long Island might never even hear about."

He made a face. "At least, that's what my parents say."

"But you'll be *gone*!" Griffin protested.

"Only to New Jersey. I'll be able to come home some weekends."

The pavement seemed to sway under Griffin's feet. "That's not good enough! What's the point of having a best friend if you only get him 'some weekends'? Do you want us to end up like Luthor, dragging around the house, lower than a caterpillar, barely able to scrape up the energy to bite the cable guy?"

Ben sat down on the curbstone, staring glumly at the scuffed toes of his sneakers. "You think I *want* to go to that dumb school? But if my folks say I have to, what can I do about it?"

Griffin was offended. "How can you of all people ask me that question? First, we come up with a plan. . . ."

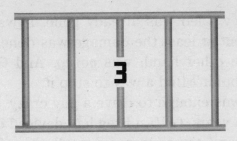

3

PROBLEM: Ben might have to go to the DuPont Youth Academy for Sleep Science.

OBJECTIVE: Stop this AT ALL COSTS!!!

STEP ONE . . .

G riffin stared at the blank page on his desk at school. He'd started this plan in English class, and now math and social studies had come and gone. And here he was in science at progress point zero.

Not a word. Not a thought. Not even a doodle.

It was worse than Cleopatra's disappearance — and not just because Ben wasn't a monkey. Cleo was already gone. It was too bad, but at least the damage was done. Ben, on the other hand, was *going*. And Griffin still couldn't find a way to stop it.

It was enough to drive a guy crazy. In his eleven years, Griffin Bing had devised countless plans, some big, some small. One of them had even managed to rescue a million-dollar baseball card. How could he come up empty now of all times, when his best friend hung in the balance? How could The Man With The Plan draw a blank on the most important plan of his life?

Unhappy and frustrated, he looked around the classroom. He found his gloom reflected in Ben's expression. His friend was gazing out the window, his head already in New Jersey at the academy he didn't want to attend.

Then there was Savannah, in a state of sustained outrage that the police would not accept the banana as evidence of a kidnapping. She had pulled down sixty LOST posters and replaced them with ABDUCTED ones. The stress and sleepless nights were taking their toll.

But Savannah wasn't the only classmate in a blue funk these days. Antonia Benson — who went by her rock-climbing nickname,

Pitch — was bummed because her family's trip to Devils Tower had been canceled. Mr. Benson had dropped a bowling ball on his foot, and it was too swollen to cram into a hiking boot.

Child actor Logan Kellerman was depressed because his only line had been cut from the orange juice commercial he'd finally managed to get a part in.

It was impossible to read the expression on the face of computer whiz Melissa Dukakis. The shy girl lived behind a curtain of long, stringy hair. But it was a sure thing she was frowning in there somewhere. Everyone knew she had suffered a catastrophic system meltdown. It had blacked out three blocks of the Cedarville power grid.

We're not a class, Griffin thought morosely. *We're an undertakers' convention.*

Was anyone in this whole school in a good mood?

Suddenly, the door flew open. "Hey, everybody!" announced a loud, brash voice. "Isn't it a great day?"

Linebacker-sized Darren Vader didn't just enter a room — he exploded into it, rattling windows and pens and sending loose paper wafting in all directions.

"I suppose it is for you, Darren." Mr. Martinez sighed. "I hope you have a good reason for being four hours late."

With a flourish, Darren presented his note. "Sailing lessons, Mr. M. My dad took me out on Long Island Sound."

Mr. Martinez was not impressed with this excuse. "During school hours?" he asked.

Darren shrugged. "It's too crowded on the weekends. My dad says I've got America's Cup potential. I need plenty of space to let it all hang out." He walked to his seat, elbowing Griffin as he passed. "How's it going, bushel-boy?"

Griffin saw red. "You're not allowed to talk about that!" he hissed.

Griffin's father was the creator of the SmartPick^{TM}, a high-tech fruit-picking tool. Now Mr. Bing was working on a new invention, the Rollo-Bushel. It was a two-wheeled motorized scooter with a SmartPick^{TM} dock and a bushel basket. The whole project was supposed to be top secret.

Darren took the seat beside Griffin and leaned over to whisper, "Wait a minute, NASCAR fans — what's that in the pole position? It's Jeff Gordon on a Rollo-Bushel! It only goes twelve miles an hour, but when the race is over, he can sell apples at trackside!"

Griffin swiveled in his seat. "Not another word, Vader! Just because your mom is our patent lawyer —"

"Touchy, touchy, picker-man."

"That's enough!" Mr. Martinez exclaimed. "Griffin and Darren, if you can't behave yourselves, you will *not* be joining us on the field trip to *All Aboard Animals* next week."

Savannah perked up a little. "You mean the floating zoo?"

The teacher nodded. "They're docking at the Rutherford Point Preserve, and school groups are invited to visit." He turned back to Griffin and Darren. "But if you two can't control yourselves, you will not be included."

Darren puffed a stream of hot air through a hollowed-out pen at the back of Griffin's neck.

Griffin hunkered down and concentrated his attention on the plan.

STEP ONE. . .

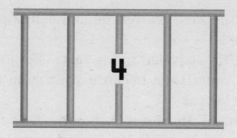

4

The Rutherford Point Preserve was located on a neck of land on the North Shore of Long Island. Back in the 1800s, it had been a waterfront estate belonging to multimillionaire oil tycoon Beaumont Rutherford. He had bequeathed the property to the state of New York to use as a park.

The place's history as a rich man's hideaway was very much in evidence as the Cedarville school bus circled the twenty-five-foot-high wrought-iron fence and entered through the towering front gate.

Even Darren was impressed. "Whoa! I'm going to get myself a place like this when I get rich and leave you losers in the dust!"

Mr. Martinez laughed tolerantly. "You'd better start saving now, Darren. Remember why the Rutherford family had to give it away. Even *they* couldn't afford to pay the taxes."

Darren shrugged. "So I'll invent the Dumb-Pick or something like that. How hard can it be?"

Griffin was about to whack Darren with his lunch bag when he noticed that Ben had dozed off in the seat beside him. The timing of this field trip had thrown off his friend's corrective nap schedule.

"Wake up, man!" Griffin hissed, with a sharp elbow to Ben's ribs.

Ben's head bobbled upright. "I'm awake!" He peered out the window. "Wow, look at this place!"

The main house was a gray stone castle, complete with turrets and towering balconies.

Melissa peered through her hair curtain. "Is that the zoo?"

"Nice crib!" Darren exclaimed. "I wish *I* was an animal!"

"You are," Griffin pointed out. "A pig."

"That's not fair," Savannah protested. "Pigs are highly intelligent, sensitive creatures."

"*All Aboard Animals* is a *floating* zoo," Mr. Martinez reminded them. "Look, everybody —"

The bus crested a rise, and the gleaming waters of Long Island Sound stretched out before them. Moored at the wooden wharf was a large boat that resembled a Mississippi River steamer, long and rectangular, with a paddle wheel at the stern.

The bus parked behind two others, and Mr. Martinez led his students down the path onto the dock. As they waited for the class ahead of them to file down the gangway, Griffin noted that the paddle-wheel steamer didn't look quite as spiffy as it had from a distance. The paint that wasn't peeling was considerably faded. And close up they could see that the pictures of jungle cats, elephants, and giraffes on the hull were merely decals.

Savannah was frowning. "No way is there a giraffe on this ship. Even a baby would have its head sticking right through the roof. And an elephant? It would probably break through the deck."

Finally, it was their turn to go aboard. The first thing Griffin noticed as he stepped inside the hatch was an overpowering foul smell. Heads retreated into shoulders; fingers came up to hold noses.

As usual, Darren was the first to find his very nasal voice. "Ugh! What hit this place — a stink bomb the size of California?"

Only Savannah was unaffected. "What a bunch of babies. Animals have a smell, just like people do. We just don't notice our own. But," she added disapprovingly, "it's possible that the cages aren't being cleaned as often as they should be."

The interior of the paddleboat was cramped, airless, and badly lit. They were greeted by Mr. Nastase, the manager. He was a tall, cadaverous man in a hand-tailored suit with shirt cuffs that set off his impeccable manicure. Even his haircut looked expensive.

"Welcome to *All Aboard Animals*," he intoned. "You stand on the threshold of an incredible adventure. . . ." His speech was dramatic, but it was obvious he'd given it ten thousand times, and it bored him mightily.

Savannah couldn't hold back her curiosity. She waved her hand right under his pointed nose, but he ignored her, studiously focusing on a rivet in the bulkhead behind the class. Finally, she blurted out, "Mr. Nastase, exactly what kind of animals do you have here?"

"I'm glad you asked me that," the zoo-keeper deadpanned, smoothing down a thin mustache that was shaped like the apex of the Great Pyramid and looking anything but glad. "You will see animals that will astound you, animals from the four corners of the earth. . . ." He droned on for some time about what they were going to see. When it was over, he still hadn't mentioned a single animal.

Even Mr. Martinez was becoming impatient with the man. "How about a little hint?" he asked.

Mr. Nastase drew himself up to a tall, gaunt height. "I will not spoil your voyage of discovery." He disappeared into a small cabin marked OFFICE.

The class followed Mr. Martinez through a low hatch and gathered around the first exhibit. There, a dim bulb cast a yellowish glow into a small mesh cage. Inside cowered a beady-eyed furry creature that would have fit in the palm of any of their hands.

"A chipmunk?" Pitch exclaimed in disbelief. "I almost stepped on one of these on the way to school this morning! This is from the four corners of my yard, not the four corners of the *earth*."

Savannah shushed her sharply. "Animals may not speak our language, but they can sense if you don't respect them. He has feelings, you know."

"This is only the first exhibit," soothed Mr. Martinez. "I'm sure they have more exciting things to show us. Let's reserve judgment until we've seen the entire collection."

They continued their tour of the paddle-wheel steamer and its caged exhibits. The closer they got to the heart of the ship, the more the smells and the stale air intensified.

There were some interesting animals — a meerkat, a prairie dog, a chuckwalla, and a great horned owl, which opened one big yellow eye and looked baleful at their interruption. But they all seemed undersized and listless. And the rest of the collection was incredibly ordinary, an assortment of hamsters, frogs, garter snakes, turtles, mice, and a ferret that was either very young or just plain puny. A sickly chicken marched nervously around a cage marked FARM ANIMALS, next door to a skin-and-bones piglet.

The class wandered among the displays in stunned silence.

Ben tapped Griffin on the shoulder. "Is it just me, or is this place really, really lame?"

"This place would have to rise up five hundred percent to improve to lame," Griffin agreed. "Look at Mr. Martinez. I don't think he's too thrilled."

"Never mind him," said Ben. "Check out Savannah."

Savannah Drysdale was so outraged that she actually radiated heat. She darted from cage to cage, and each new discovery twisted her face further out of shape.

"This habitat hasn't been cleaned in days!" she seethed. "The water is dirty and brackish! The ferret cage is half the size it should be! How can a growing baby develop muscle tone without room enough to turn around? The meerkat and chuckwalla need extra heat! The loon barely has a feather left! The beaver is high and dry!"

Griffin stepped in front of her. "Savannah — take a breath —"

"I'm not going to breathe!" she insisted. "None of the animals can breathe in this torture chamber! Why should *we* breathe?"

At that moment, Mr. Nastase appeared

beside the owl enclosure. "Is there a problem?"

"This whole place is a problem!" Savannah couldn't hold herself back — she was genuinely fuming. "It's too dark; it's not properly ventilated; the animals are neglected, undernourished —"

"I'm sure you're mistaken, young lady," the zookeeper said stiffly, his deep frown forming the lines of his mustache into an arrowhead. "Perhaps you'll be happier with our newest addition, our pride and joy." He led the group through a hatch to a smaller cabin, which held a single cage.

Griffin could already hear the sound of wild scrambling from within that enclosure, followed by excited animal chatter.

The scream that came from Savannah was barely human.

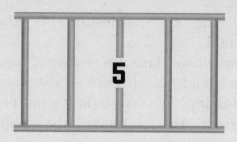

*"C*leo!!"
      Savannah bounded across the cabin and pressed her face against the mesh of the cage. The capuchin monkey nuzzled up to her, screeching wildly.

"It's okay, sweetie. I'm here." She wheeled on the zookeeper, eyes shooting sparks. "What are you doing with my monkey?"

His mustache was nearly two vertical lines. "There must be a misunderstanding. Eleanor is our latest attraction at *All Aboard Animals.*"

"She's not Eleanor, she's Cleopatra! And she's *mine!*"

"My dear —"

"I'm not your dear! You stole my monkey!"

Mr. Martinez stepped between them. "What's going on here? Savannah — you had a monkey?"

"She even got a traffic ticket," Ben put in helpfully.

"I *still* have her!" Savannah insisted. "She's right here! Can't you see how she responds to me?"

"Capuchins are excitable," Mr. Nastase lectured. "Of course Eleanor became agitated when you pressed so close to the cage. You were invading her space. You obviously have a lot to learn about animals."

A gasp went up from the class. At age eleven, Savannah knew more about animals than most zoology professors did.

She turned anxiously to her teacher. "Mr. Martinez, aren't you going to help me? This floating dungeon has no right to keep Cleopatra! She's mine!"

Mr. Martinez looked profoundly disturbed. "Are you absolutely sure of this?"

"Yes! A hundred percent!"

"That's not possible," Mr. Nastase said confidently. "Eleanor has been with us for months. We have the paperwork — a bill of sale — to prove it. All capuchins look alike, and there are no distinguishing marks or physical abnormalities on Eleanor. I sympathize that you seem to have lost your own monkey, dear girl, but she is not our Eleanor."

"Not true!" Savannah stormed. "You stole Cleo right out of my yard!"

Mr. Martinez was at a complete loss about what to do. "He has a bill of sale —"

"So he says," Savannah scoffed. "I haven't seen it. And even if I do see it, I won't believe it, because it'll be fake!"

Mr. Nastase made an elaborate show of checking his watch. "My goodness, where did the time go? Oh, yes, it was wasted on slander and accusation. Your tour is over." His brow clouded menacingly. "Now."

Savannah looked beseechingly at her teacher, but Mr. Martinez shook his head sadly. "I want to help you, but the school can't get involved with this. You'll have to talk to your parents."

"Cleo can't stay here!" Savannah protested. "This place is a germ factory! She'll get sick! All these poor animals will, if they're not sick already!" She grabbed the door of the monkey's cage and began to heave on it. A padlock held it in place. In growing agitation, she tried to pick up the entire cage. It was bolted to the bulkhead and wouldn't budge.

The zookeeper watched her with alarm. "*Klaus!*" he called.

The man who came running was at least a man and a half, with huge hands and enormous feet. Size 22 construction boots pounded the deck with every step.

"Escort our guests ashore, please," Mr. Nastase ordered. "And make sure they get back on their bus."

Klaus frowned at the clock. "There's still twenty minutes to go," he rumbled in a voice that sounded like it was coming from the bottom of a well.

"Not for this lot," the zookeeper said coldly. "They've already caused disturbance enough."

Mr. Martinez gently but firmly pulled Savannah off the cage. Klaus began herding the visitors back through the exhibits toward the gangway.

As they disembarked, they must have appeared totally cowed, because they drew stares from the student group waiting to go in next.

"You guys are in for a treat," Darren assured them.

Savannah seemed to be planning a bull run back onto the paddleboat. "I can't leave her!"

Mr. Martinez held on to her arm. "I understand you're upset," he said firmly. "But maybe you were seeing Cleopatra there because you wanted it to be her. Going back will only create more of a scene."

Savannah shuffled and looked torn, offering neither excuse nor apology.

The uncomfortable silence was broken by Griffin. "Mr. Martinez, I don't know much about monkeys, but I know Savannah. If she says that's Cleopatra, that's good enough for me."

Ben stepped forward. "Me, too."

"They're right," said Pitch. "There's no way that Mr. Nasty understands animals like Savannah. He's got the crummiest zoo I've ever seen!"

One by one, the students all expressed support for their classmate. Her record as an animal expert spoke for itself.

Even Darren was supportive. "Much as I hate to agree with these knuckleheads, my money's on Drysdale. That guy jacked the monkey."

All this only served to make Mr. Martinez feel more defensive. "I'm not disagreeing with any of you. But I'm not a policeman, and the school is not the Supreme Court. Savannah, you're going to have to take this up with your parents. They'll decide what to do."

Savannah was silent as the class boarded their bus for the drive back to Cedarville. Her eyes never left the scratched window and, beyond that, the paddleboat, where she knew Cleopatra was being held captive.

Griffin watched her, a gnawing feeling deep in his stomach. Mr. Nastase said no, so it was no. Mr. Martinez said no, so it was no. Didn't Savannah have rights?

Beside him, Ben let out a tremulous yawn.

Did any kid?

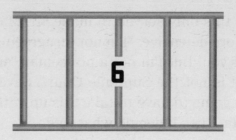

The SmartPick™ Rollo-Bushel threaded its way through the obstacle course of orange cones that its inventor had set up in the garage.

Mr. Bing came to a halt and hopped off, looking pleased with himself. "You see? The platform swivels so it's more maneuverable in the tight space of an orchard."

Griffin sat on one of the other prototypes that were lined up against the back wall. "Awesome, Dad," he said listlessly.

His father's brow clouded. "So why doesn't Daria Vader see that? She's dragging her feet on submitting the paperwork. She thinks the Rollo-Bushel needs to be more unique to get approved by the patent office."

Griffin didn't look up. "Great . . . great . . ."

Mr. Bing frowned. "Guess I'm not the only one with problems." He perched on the workbench beside his son. "All right, out with it."

"Oh, nothing," Griffin mumbled. "I was just, you know, thinking."

Mr. Bing nodded. "I talked to Mr. Slovak last night —" Griffin looked up in surprise. "Yeah, I have a life, too. I don't spend all my time in here with my nose buried in electric motors. You're worried about Ben going away to boarding school, right?"

"It's not fair, Dad. Nobody asked him if he wants to go to some academy in New Jersey."

His father raised an eyebrow. "Did it ever occur to you that Ben *needs* that academy?"

"He *doesn't* need it!" Griffin insisted hotly. "He's doing fine. He takes a fifteen-minute nap at school every day, and he's as awake as anybody. None of the kids even know about it. They think he goes to the nurse for allergy meds."

Mr. Bing nodded. "You're right. Ben's not doing too badly — now. But no one stays eleven forever. What if he can't drive a car because he might fall asleep at the wheel? What if the condition gets worse? Ben is going to have a completely normal life with no limits, but it might take some doing. He can't pass up the chance to work with the very top people in that field."

Griffin was too unhappy to be logical. Dad could talk from today until tomorrow and make it seem like the most sensible thing in the world, but there was only one reason why Ben was going to this dumb sleep school: because he didn't have the power to say no. He was a kid in an adult world, and that was a powerless thing to be.

There was a tapping at the metal door, and Mrs. Bing poked her head into the garage. "Griffin, your friend Savannah is waiting for you in the den."

"Thanks." He followed his mother into the house. It was the day of the big meeting. The Drysdales had gone to see their lawyer in New York City to talk about Cleopatra and how to get the monkey back. They had been unable to identify "Eleanor" as Savannah's missing pet during their own visit to the floating zoo. But they had complete faith in their daughter's knowledge of animals. Everybody did.

Savannah sat on the couch watching *Shark Week*, an expression of deep distaste on her delicate features. "It never ceases to amaze me what people will do to make money off animals," she complained. "They're acting like sharks are *dangerous* just to get high ratings for their TV show."

"Never mind that," said Griffin. "How did it go with the lawyer?"

Her face crumpled, and for the first time he noticed the circles around her eyes. "I think Cleo's going to have to live on that awful boat."

Griffin was horrified. "The lawyer said that?"

She nodded miserably. "He said a bill of sale is legally binding unless I can prove that Cleo is mine."

"So prove it, then!" Griffin insisted. "Call that friend of yours — the animal scientist!"

"Dr. Kathleen Alford. She's Curator of the Long Island Zoo."

"Surely she knows how to identify a stolen monkey!"

Savannah shook her head sadly. "I tried that. Dr. Alford said the only way to prove that Eleanor is really Cleopatra is through DNA. I'd have to go through her blanket and find a few of her hairs. Then I'd have to send them away to a lab. It takes weeks and costs thousands of dollars. Even then, we've still got nothing unless we can match it to a DNA sample from the real Cleopatra — like Mr. Nasty's going to give us permission for that. We'd have to get a court order. Even if we won, it would take over a year. Cleo is a gentle, sensitive creature who thrives on companionship and love. Who knows if she could even survive that kind of mistreatment for so long?" Tears streamed down her cheeks. "You've got to help me, Griffin! I don't know what's left to try!"

Griffin stared in genuine alarm. This was Savannah, tamer of Luthor. Where animals were concerned, she was the toughest kid in town. He couldn't remember ever seeing her cry before.

"What can I do?" he said honestly. "What do I know about monkeys that you don't?"

"But you're the guy who gets things done! The Man With The Plan!"

The more Griffin thought about it, the more it drove him crazy. This should have been a no-brainer. Cleopatra was missing, and Cleopatra had been found. Happy reunion, right? Wrong. Standing in the way of justice: a procession of adults — Mr. Nasty, Klaus, Mr. Martinez, lab people, lawyers, even

Savannah's own parents, telling her it couldn't be done.

It was the Ben thing all over again — kids' lives being jerked around by the adult world.

Savannah grabbed his arm, hanging on like a drowning sailor. "I wouldn't ask if it was just for me, Griffin. We need a plan to save Cleopatra!"

"But — she's just —"

"Just a monkey?" Savannah finished angrily.

Griffin shut his mouth and sealed it. That was exactly what he'd been about to say. And saying it to Savannah was a good way to be fed to Luthor.

Savannah's face flamed red. "So it's okay for her to be kidnapped and held against her will? Why, if Cleo was a person, the police would send the SWAT team to storm the zoo boat and rescue her!"

"Too bad there's no SWAT team for animals," Griffin put in lamely.

Savannah was resentful. "Well, there should be."

And suddenly, as it was with all truly great plans, Operation Zoobreak appeared, fully formed, in Griffin's imagination.

7

"What's a zoobreak?" Ben asked in bewilderment.

"Shhh!" Griffin looked around. The two were in the middle of the parade of Cedarville kids heading to school the next morning, but nobody appeared to be eavesdropping. "I came up with it, but it was based on something Savannah said. Think prison break, only with animals."

Ben stared at him. "You mean busting the monkey out of the zoo boat? You're not serious! No, I take that back. You're *always* serious."

"I'm no animal nut like Savannah," Griffin said evenly, "but how can we leave Cleopatra there? She'll end up skinny and moth-eaten like every other animal on that garbage barge! Besides, Savannah's our friend."

Ben was adamant. "Yeah, I feel bad for her, too. But this — is it even possible?"

"*Everything* is possible," Griffin lectured, "if you've got the right plan."

"Come on, Griffin, we're just kids —" No sooner had the words passed Ben's lips than he wished he could cram them back down his throat. This was the last argument that would ever work on his best friend.

Griffin drew himself up to his full height, towering over Ben. "I know a bunch of kids who were swindled out of a million-dollar baseball card. And you know what those 'just kids' did? They put together a plan and took back what was rightfully theirs! We did that on our own, and we can do it for Cleopatra. It's the same thing."

"It's *not* the same thing!" Ben argued. "The Babe Ruth card was right here in Cedarville! The Rutherford Point Preserve is miles away. Not to mention that we could have gone to jail for that Babe Ruth card and almost got killed about fifteen different ways."

"I never said it wasn't going to be hard," Griffin reasoned.

Ben looked miserable. "You know I have problems. If I get caught boosting a monkey, that's just one more reason for my parents to think I'd be better off at boarding school. I can't get mixed up in anything like this."

Griffin grew solemn. "That's exactly why you *have* to get mixed up in this. Don't you see? It could be the very last chance for the two of us to work on a plan together."

Ben shook his head. "You don't fight fair!"

Griffin jumped on this. "So you're in?"

At last, Ben nodded reluctantly. "But we're going to need a lot of help. There's no way you, me, and Savannah can do it on our own."

Griffin smiled. "It's time to get the team back together."

8

OPERATION ZOOBREAK

THE TEAM:

ANTONIA "PITCH" BENSON

Specialty – climbing
Objective – scale 25-foot fence

Griffin and Ben motioned Pitch down from her usual spot at the summit of the climbing apparatus in the gym.

"I'll have to take another look around the preserve," she told them after hearing the plan. "I can probably get myself over. The rest of you might be a problem."

Griffin nodded. "We're working on finding someone to take us back to the preserve on the weekend. We'll need to do more scouting before we can finalize the plan."

Pitch grinned. "My dad is bored stiff because he's off climbing till the swelling goes down. I'll bet I can talk him into driving us."

MELISSA DUKAKIS

Specialty – computers and high tech

Objective – electronic surveillance of <u>All Aboard Animals</u>

The lights flickered in the computer lab as Melissa downloaded the new software she had designed at home. She agitated her head, parting her stringy hair to reveal eyes wide with wonder. "And you want *me* to help?"

"Nobody knows more about technology," Griffin told her. "At least, not around here. How can we spy on the zoo boat?"

Melissa stared into the distance for what seemed like a long time. Finally, she said a single word: "webcams."

Griffin jumped on this. "You mean we plant them around Rutherford Point?"

"How would we plug them in?" asked Ben.

"They make wireless ones with built-in transmitters," Melissa explained. "The batteries last a week. Can we act fast?"

"We have to," Griffin informed her. *"All Aboard Animals* sets sail for their next location on April tenth. The clock is already ticking."

LOGAN KELLERMAN

Specialty – acting

Objective – Klaus control

"Control *that* guy?" Logan was so shocked that he stepped out of the spotlight, something that almost never happened. "I'm an actor, not a sumo wrestler!"

Griffin and Ben hustled him off the stage and into the wings.

"You don't have to fight him," Griffin soothed. "You just have to get to know him. When we go to scope out *All Aboard Animals* on Saturday, you use your acting skill to get his attention, and then you find out as much as you can about the security on the boat after hours."

Logan was relieved. "I can do that. In fact, I'm beginning to feel the role coming to me."

"Don't get too fancy," Ben advised. "He's a muscle head, not an idiot. You don't want him to guess what we're up to."

"Shhh!" Logan hissed. "I'm getting into character. My childhood has been painful. . . ."

"It's going to be a lot more painful if you get Klaus mad at you," Griffin warned.

"Don't worry, you guys," Logan promised. "You can count on me. This is going to be an Academy Award performance."

"Come on, Kellerman," the spotlight operator called in annoyance. "You're supposed to stand on your *X*."

"Don't rush me!" Logan snapped. His acting skill faced far greater challenges than one little school play.

Luthor's supper dish was the size of a slop sink, and Savannah filled it from a bag of dog food taller than she was.

"Cleo doesn't need *handling*," she told them. "You're never going to find a more mature, well-behaved primate."

It was feeding time in Savannah's room, which was a major operation. The cats, rabbits, turtles, parakeet, and chameleon were already chowing down with gusto. Only Luthor showed no interest in his meal, gazing with sadness at the empty bowl marked CLEOPATRA.

Griffin grinned at Savannah. "In that case, why don't you just stay home, and we'll stuff her in a gunnysack and drag her off the boat?"

"I will be there," Savannah insisted emotionally, "to whisper in her ear that it's all going to be okay."

"And that's not handling?" asked Ben.

"It's friendship and support at a time when she needs it most. Poor Cleo! She's been kidnapped and held hostage on that floating sewer! Even though we're rescuing her, it'll still be traumatic. Monkeys can be very easily stressed. Everyone knows that."

Griffin rolled his eyes. "So I'll cross out 'handler' and put in 'guidance counselor.' Come on, Savannah, we're on the same side here!"

She reddened. "Sorry, Griffin. You guys are awesome for doing this. I'm never going to forget it, and neither is Cleo!"

BEN SLOVAK

Specialty – smallest kid in town
Objective – sneaking onto boat via tight space

"Aw, Griffin, why do I always have to be the tight-spaces guy? You don't even know if *All Aboard Animals* has any tight spaces!"

Griffin and Ben headed down Savannah's

front walk, with Luthor's dejected whining still ringing in their ears.

"I'm sure they lock the boat up at night," Griffin explained. "You can't predict the exact details, but we need a kid shrimpy enough to jam through a porthole just in case. Besides, I want someone on the team I trust with my life, someone to be my assistant."

"Assistant to what?" Ben challenged. "Melissa's webcams spy on the boat; Logan neutralizes the security guy; Pitch gets us onto the grounds; I crawl on board and let everybody else in; Savannah takes her monkey home. The only person who doesn't have a job is *you*, Griffin. What do you do on this team?"

GRIFFIN BING

Specialty – burglary

Objective – springing monkey from cage

Possible BREAK-IN methods:

(i) pick lock (school library has no burglary books; check public)

(ii) burn opening with blowtorch (how flammable is monkey fur?)

(iii) wire cutters (thickness of bars?!)

That night, the team in place, Griffin sat back at his desk and studied his notes in a businesslike fashion. It wasn't a plan — not yet. He had formulated enough plans to know that the details would not come together until their scouting trip to the Rutherford Point Preserve on Saturday.

Hang in there, Cleo, he thought to himself. *It won't be long now.*

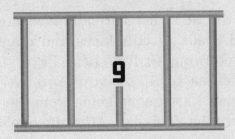

9

"This must be some zoo to have you kids begging to come back so soon."

Nick Benson, Pitch's father, piloted his Land Cruiser in through the gates of the Rutherford Point Preserve.

"It definitely caught our interest," his daughter agreed, her sharp eyes scanning the wrought-iron fence poles from ground level to their lancelike points.

As Pitch had predicted, it hadn't taken much convincing to get her father to act as chauffeur for the scouting mission on Saturday. Sidelined from climbing by his swollen foot, he was anxious to divert his mind from the fact that he was not in Wyoming, hanging off a rope at the seven-hundred-foot mark of Devils Tower.

So the SUV that normally navigated the rugged roads to cliff faces and crags was now returning Griffin, Ben, Pitch, Logan, and Melissa to *All Aboard Animals*. Only Savannah was staying home from this stage of Operation Zoobreak. After the unpleasant scene at the field trip, she couldn't risk being recognized by Mr. Nastase.

"We should split up, too," Griffin whispered in the backseat. "Together, we might jog the guy's memory."

In the parking lot, Mr. Benson limped to a bench and settled himself down with a book. The team made a great show of heading for the zoo boat. But Pitch left the others and doubled back across the manicured lawn to have a closer look at the fence around the property.

Melissa reached into her pocket and produced four tiny battery-powered wireless webcams. The purpose of these cameras was to give the team a complete view of what happened when *All Aboard Animals* shut down and locked up for the night. Griffin's plan called for her to plant them where they would provide different angles.

She surveyed the dock area thoughtfully, determined to get this exactly right.

She wanted to do her part to help rescue Cleopatra, but there was more to it than that. Melissa was a loner, more comfortable with computers than with actual living people. Before the baseball card heist, she'd never had any friends. She didn't want to let the team down. The thought that she was being asked to help again was almost too good to be true.

The first vantage point was in a maple tree with a straight-on view of the starboard side of the paddleboat and the main gangway. She picked a wad of chewing gum out of her mouth and used it as mortar to set the tiny camera in place in the crook of a branch.

The second spot was atop a pylon on the dock itself. It focused on the zoo boat's bow and was also set in gum. The third she positioned for a view of the stern, not dead-on, but at an angle that also provided another view of the entrance.

That was enough, she thought. There was still one webcam left. She looked around for Griffin. He was in line on the gangway, waiting to get into the exhibit. There was no chance to talk to him now. And the rule was to stay separated.

She made an executive decision. She would place the final webcam aboard the boat, monitoring the entrance from the inside.

As she headed for the gangway, she popped another stick of gum into her mouth and began to chew.

Griffin was standing in line to buy his ticket when he made his first Nastase sighting. The zookeeper was manning the cash box and stamping hands.

Griffin caught a nervous look from Ben, three people ahead of him. But he was relieved to see his friend hand over his twelve dollars and pass through without a second glance.

Twelve bucks to look at a bunch of moth-eaten squirrels and a stolen monkey — all while being drenched in the stink of poorly maintained cages. This guy was a big-time crook.

Now it was Griffin's turn. The zookeeper paused, his squinty black eyes riveted to Griffin's face, his expression saying: *Where have I seen you before?*

Griffin felt a stab of fear. He had been the first to speak up for Savannah on field trip day. After her, he might be the easiest for Mr. Nastase to recognize.

He held out his hand with twelve dollar bills fanned out like playing cards.

The money broke the spell. "Welcome to *All Aboard Animals*," the zookeeper greeted in a bored tone. "Prepare to be astounded."

Griffin nodded, shaken, and fled past. He caught up with Ben at the chipmunk cage.

"What was that all about?" Ben hissed. "Did he remember you?"

"I think he was starting to," Griffin whispered back. "I threw him off the scent with a fistful of dollars. Come on, let's find Cleopatra."

They navigated quickly through the depressing display of ill-kept and underweight animals, gagging as the stench grew stronger toward the center of the ship. To make matters even more unpleasant, a group of smirking teenagers had gathered around the great horned owl, rattling the cage every time the nocturnal bird tried to close its eyes. The earsplitting hoot-shriek echoed all through the paddleboat.

"Savannah wouldn't like that," Ben observed.

. "Savannah doesn't like anything about

this place," Griffin replied. "Look, there's Cleopatra."

The monkey was in the same separate compartment. The only new addition was a hand-lettered sign that declared:

PRESENTING: THE LADY ELEANOR

They hung back as a mom and two little kids, one a toddler in her arms, made monkey sounds and fawned over Mr. Nastase's latest exhibit. At last, the family moved on, allowing Griffin and Ben to get close to Cleopatra.

In the few days since the class trip, the capuchin had undergone an alarming transformation. There was only one word to describe the poor creature — depressed. The climber and swinger who had made best friends with the toughest Doberman in Cedarville had become a silent, drooping figure. She squatted in the cage, seemingly unconnected to the world around her, eaten up by her own sadness.

Griffin sidled up to the enclosure and slipped a couple of pieces of sliced plantain between the bars. "These are from Savannah," he whispered. "Eat them fast, before somebody notices." He felt like an idiot, talking to the monkey as if she were a human being. But he had promised Savannah to deliver her message. "Don't lose hope. Your friends haven't forgotten you. And — oh, yeah — Luthor says hey."

It might have been just their imagination, but Cleopatra seemed to perk up a little bit. She definitely enjoyed the plantains.

"What do you think about the cage?" Ben ventured.

"Wire cutters. Definitely. The bars aren't too thick. The big question is how to get in here if the boat's locked down." He cast a quick glance around the compartment, his eyes coming to rest on a ventilation grate in the ceiling.

Ben followed his gaze in alarm. "You mean *me*? You want me to climb in through that thing?"

Griffin nodded. "And then let the rest of us in the front door."

"Aw, Griffin, couldn't we just wait till nobody's watching, cut Cleopatra loose, and make a run for it?"

Griffin was horrified. "In the middle of all these people, with Klaus around and Mr. Nasty watching the door? That's the worst plan I've ever heard in my life! Even if we do get off the boat, they can stop us at the main gate of the preserve. Somebody's bound to notice the missing monkey by then!"

"It was just a thought," Ben mumbled, chastened. "You're the one who said a plan is never finished until you've considered all the possibilities."

"A nighttime assault is our only option," Griffin stated with certainty. "The big question is, can you fit into that vent?"

"An amoeba couldn't fit into that vent," Ben replied bitterly.

"Only one way to find out, I guess," said Griffin, as if Ben had never spoken. "We just have to find the outside opening for those ducts. Come on. We've had our twenty-four bucks worth."

They retraced their steps to the entrance, arriving just in time to receive a discreet nod from Melissa. The webcams were in place.

Mr. Nastase barely looked up from the cash box as Griffin and Ben left the exhibit. The zookeeper took no notice when, instead of exiting via the gangway, they made a quick left turn and hurried along the paddleboat's narrow outer deck.

Ben bit his lip. "I don't know about this. All the people in line saw us run off where we're not supposed to be."

Griffin walked briskly ahead. "Don't worry about them," he advised, scanning the superstructure of the ship for possible vent openings. "Mr. Nasty's inside counting his money. He's the one who can't know where we are."

"*And* Klaus," Ben added.

Another left turn brought them to the stern of the ship, which housed the paddle wheel. The deck was wider, but they had to pick their way around coils of rope and piles of equipment. There were no air vents on the superstructure, just three steel-rimmed portholes. One of these provided a view of the owl and its teenage tormentors. Klaus had arrived on the scene, gesturing emphatically with muscular arms thick as tree trunks.

Ben was terrified. "Let's scram before he looks out the window!"

"Not until we find the vent," Griffin replied stubbornly. "Hey —"

Ben followed his friend's pointing finger. A hornlike shape protruded from the roof.

"I'll bet that's it," Griffin decided.

Ben wasn't convinced. "Looks more like a tuba."

The two explored the rest of the starboard side and the bow. There were no other openings.

Griffin returned to the big horn. "This has to be it. Come on, I'll give you a boost."

"I can't climb in there now! The boat's full of people!"

"You don't have to go inside. Just get up there and make sure the opening's big enough." He laced his fingers together, forming a stirrup.

With a tremulous sigh, Ben grabbed his friend's shoulder and then stepped onto Griffin's interlocked hands. Griffin heaved, straightening his back and raising Ben upward. The smaller boy reached for a handhold, but he was still shy of the roof. With a whimper, he toppled onto Griffin. The two of them ended up in a heap on the deck.

Ben rubbed a bruised knee. "First rule of boosting: Make sure the booster can get the boostee high enough."

"We're just a few inches short." Griffin looked around determinedly. "Jackpot!" He scrambled astern and returned lugging a heavy fluorescent yellow suitcase marked DANGER.

Ben was alarmed. "Put that down! It could be a bomb!"

"It's not a bomb, it's a life raft," Griffin explained. "Nothing happens if you don't pull the cord."

He slid the heavy case along the deck until it lay directly underneath the vent opening. Then he stepped onto it and formed the foothold once again. "Okay, round two."

The extra twelve inches made the difference. Ben was able to get his hands on the edge of the roof and, with Griffin pushing from below, scrambled up beside the horn. He peered into the bell. "It's the vent, all right," he called back. "There's a grill over it — four screws. Looks pretty tight —"

"Can you get inside?" Griffin asked.

Ben dearly wished he could have said no. But there was no sense trying to discourage Griffin. It never happened. He'd just find another way in, probably through the bilge pump.

He sighed unhappily. "I'll fit."

10

L ogan Kellerman was acting.

No, that didn't even come close to describing it. He was completely in character, just as he had been for the orange juice commercial: It didn't matter that Boise's Grovestand tasted like toxic waste — those Idaho guys should probably stick to potatoes. It had taken a true actor to announce, "This is the best orange juice I've ever had!" and really *sell* the line.

He toured through the cages of *All Aboard Animals*, drinking in the sights through the eyes of his character, the sounds through the ears of his character, and the smells through the nose of his character.

There was only one problem. Where was his audience? Where was Klaus? He couldn't very well knock on the office door and ask for the security guard.

What would Johnny Depp do?

A mountain of a man with a shock of platinum blond hair appeared, herding three teenagers to the exit. Hooray! The performance was saved!

At six-foot-seven, 295 pounds, Klaus Anthony wasn't expecting trouble from the teens, and he didn't get any. He escorted the owl tormentors past the waiting crowd on the gangway and let his massive bodybuilder frame do the talking.

Klaus prided himself on being a man of few words.

When he reentered the zoo boat, he nearly tripped over Logan, who was seated on the deck by the chipmunk cage, his back against the bulkhead, his face buried in his hands in an attitude of utter misery.

"You can't sit here, kid," Klaus rumbled.

Logan looked up to reveal red-rimmed eyes and a tragic expression. "But I'm so *sad*!" he quavered, stretching the word into several syllables.

Klaus was unmoved. "Be sad somewhere else," he grunted, and walked off into the exhibit.

Logan watched, frowning, as the big man disappeared through the hatch. Hmmm. This was going to be a tougher gig than he'd thought.

Okay, time to take out the heavy artillery. The greatest test of an actor was crying. Logan was confident he could weep as well as any of the biggest stars in Hollywood.

He caught up with the burly security man at the farm animals exhibit, repairing a gap in the chicken wire that separated the hen from the piglet. Logan entered bawling, giving it all he had. The performance was a tour de force. Each full-throated sob threatened to suck the stagnant air out of the cabin. If the Boise's Grovestand people had seen this, they never would have cut his line. They might even have made him their *spokesperson*.

A few customers came over to see what the matter was, but Klaus simply said, "If you cry on the animals, I'm going to have to ask you to leave," and ducked through the hatch to another compartment. A moment later, Logan spied his sturdy frame through a porthole, inspecting the paddleboat's outer deck.

"I'm fine," he assured the small crowd that had gathered. "I just — uh — stubbed my toe." It wasn't very good acting, but these people were not the real audience.

Okay, Logan thought to himself. A performer who couldn't win over the critics would never get anywhere in show business.

He ran out of the zoo and followed Klaus aft along the narrow deck. When the moment was right, he rushed around the corner to the stern and called, "Hey, mister!"

The big man wheeled. "You again! You're not supposed to be here —"

Just as Logan was about to launch into his well-rehearsed speech, he looked past Klaus's giant shoulder and caught sight of Griffin helping Ben down from the roof on the starboard side of the stern. Oh, no! If he couldn't hold Klaus's attention now, the security man would turn and catch them in the act.

There is a time in every actor's career when he has to throw away the script and think on his feet. For Logan Kellerman, that time was now.

He bumped against a life preserver, managing to hip-check it off its hook on the rail. Stumbling carefully, he got his feet tangled up in it. With a pitiful cry for help, he heaved himself over the side and hit the cold water with a resounding splash. There he floundered, thrashing and spitting, obviously in grave danger of drowning.

Shocked, Klaus snatched up the life preserver and tossed it overboard. It hit the water three feet from Logan.

The actor made no attempt to go for it. If he couldn't distract Klaus long enough to allow Griffin and Ben to escape, this whole improvisation would be for nothing.

"Grab it, kid!" Klaus called down.

"I can't swim!"

"Oh, for crying out loud!" The big man kicked off his shoes and jumped over the side.

Saved.

The only clean towels aboard the paddleboat were in Klaus's cabin. The best Logan could do was dry his hair and pat his wet clothes while wayward zoo visitors peered curiously in the open hatch.

The compartment was small and spare, with a tiny bunk and a dresser built into the bulkhead. It was hard for Logan to imagine

Klaus living here. He seemed larger than the entire room.

The security guard was beyond angry. "Who's in charge of you, kid? Or were you just placed on this earth to drive me crazy?"

Logan finally found his voice. "My name is Ferris Atwater, Jr."

"Who brought you here? Where are your parents?"

"They're picking me up in an hour."

"Yeah, well, you're going to be pretty moldy by then."

Logan allowed his lower lip to quiver.

Klaus was out of patience. "Oh, don't start that again. Enough with the waterworks. What's eating you, anyway? Did the world end and nobody told me?"

That was Logan's cue. "It's my dad — Ferris Atwater, Sr.," he began, immersing himself in the character. "He wants me to be a dentist, like him, and I just know I'd hate it. It's my dream to be" — he paused for effect — "a security guard."

Klaus snorted. "You're kidding, right? You mean like me?"

"*Exactly* like you," Logan confirmed admiringly. "I mean, all these animals, this whole exhibit — none of it could happen if you weren't watching out to make sure every-thing's safe. You just saved my life today."

"Don't remind me."

"All the happiness people get out of this zoo," Logan went on. "You make that possible. What could be better?"

The big man sighed. "It's not as glamor-ous as you think. For one thing, look where I live. I have to stop breathing if I want to turn around in here. The boss is sitting pretty in a hotel onshore, while I sleep here to mind the store."

"Really?" Logan knew that was a wrinkle Griffin wasn't going to be thrilled about. "Why can't you just lock up the boat for the night?"

Klaus shrugged. "We do that, too. But these are animals, not coconuts. They have to be monitored."

"What if one of the animals needs you, but you can't hear it because you're asleep?"

Klaus smiled, warming up a little. "That's something you've got to learn if you're going to make it in the security game. You have to be a light sleeper like me. Any sign of trouble, I can be out of this bunk and over there with the cages in the blink of an eye."

Griffin was going to like that even less.

11

Pitch Benson had scratches over 80 per-cent of her body, but at least the scen-ery was nice. From her perch near the top of the perimeter fence, the Rutherford Point Preserve was truly a picture postcard — green rolling lawns and sparkling blue water.

"Hey, you! Get down from there!"

A middle-aged woman in a Parks Department uniform stood on the grass below, staring angrily up at her. Carefully, Pitch began her descent, picking her way along the iron posts and the prickly branches and limbs all around them. The twenty-five-foot barrier looked easy enough from the road. But on the preserve side, it was covered with dense overgrowth. For the past half hour, she had worked her way along the boundary, scraped by thorns and barbs, searching for a weak spot where the team might be able to get through. Nothing. These bushes and shrubs probably hadn't been pruned in the nearly two centuries since Rutherford himself had lived here. The spiky foliage was bad enough, but vines of glistening poison ivy slithered through the greenery just about everywhere. This place was better protected than an army base.

"Sorry."

The park lady watched in amazement as she clambered down and jumped to the ground. "Are you crazy? You could have broken your neck!"

"Tell me about it." Pitch tossed her hair over her shoulder as she jogged off toward *All Aboard Animals*.

She found Griffin, Ben, and Melissa by the dock. By now, the queue of people waiting to board the paddleboat stretched all the way to the parking lot. "Imagine standing in line for *that* zoo," she said. "Kind of like taking a number to see a cockroach infestation."

"Only grosser," Griffin agreed.

Melissa agitated her head, allowing her beady eyes to peer through the curtain of hair. "Where's Logan?"

"He's not back yet," Ben replied nervously. "Griffin, I've got a bad feeling about this. We sent a reject from an orange juice commercial to take on the Incredible Hulk."

"He'll be fine," Griffin said, unconcerned. "He's acting."

At that moment, a smiling Logan stepped off the gangway with none other than Klaus by his side. They shared a hearty handshake that crushed Logan's bones from knuckles to fingertips. Then, as the security man disappeared back into *All Aboard Animals*, Logan rejoined his zoobreak teammates.

Pitch stared at him. "What happened? Why are you all wet?"

"It was an improvisation."

"A *what*?" Ben blurted.

Logan explained how he'd taken a dive off the paddleboat in order to prevent Klaus from discovering Griffin and Ben.

Griffin was impressed. "That was some quick thinking, man. You might have saved the entire operation. And at the same time, you were able to get close to Klaus and learn his habits."

Logan nodded proudly. "He's a very light sleeper who hears every little peep coming from the animals."

"So how do we keep him from stopping us when we're on the boat, rescuing Cleopatra?" Ben asked.

Logan looked completely blank. "How should I know? I'm just an actor."

Griffin blew his stack. "That was the whole point of the acting job in the first place! You weren't auditioning for a starring role on Broadway; you were trying to find a way around Klaus!"

"That's going to be hard," Logan offered.

"Great," Griffin groaned. "We're back to the drawing board. How could it be worse?"

"I know how," Pitch put in mournfully. In a somber voice she reported her difficulties getting over the perimeter fence around the preserve.

"But scaling the fence is the key to everything!" Griffin smacked his forehead. "If we can't get onto the preserve, the whole plan is shot."

Pitch looked as distressed as he sounded. "Sorry, Griffin. I'm not even sure I could make it myself. The rest of you — forget it. And remember, we'd have to climb it *twice* — once on the way in and again when we're smuggling the monkey out."

Ben put a hand on Griffin's shoulder. "It's

not like the plan was totally perfect except for this. We didn't even have a way to get to the preserve on zoobreak night."

Griffin was unconsoled. "We would have figured something out. Worst comes to worst, we could have taken the bus. But now . . ." His voice trailed off.

"We should go," Pitch announced. From the parking lot, Mr. Benson was waving and beckoning.

Her father seemed surprised by the procession of long faces as he loaded the Land Cruiser. "I guess the zoo was kind of a disappointment the second time around." He frowned at the soggy Logan. "What happened to you?"

"They were hosing down a squirrel, and he got caught in the crossfire," Pitch told him.

The back of the SUV was a very quiet place as Mr. Benson drove up the winding road that led to the gate of the preserve.

"So I guess the plan's off, right?" Ben whispered, hoping Griffin wouldn't detect the relief in his voice.

"The plan's *never* off," Griffin hissed back stubbornly. "There's always another way — a possibility we haven't thought of yet."

"You can't pull a zoobreak if you can't get to the zoo," Ben reasoned. "The only way to reach *All Aboard Animals* is from the preserve."

Suddenly, the road veered to the right, and the complete picture was laid out before them — the dock, the paddleboat, and the sparkling blue of Long Island Sound.

Griffin squeezed Ben's forearm hard enough to splinter bone. "You're wrong. There's another approach to that ship. By water."

"You're nuts!" Logan exclaimed in a low voice. "What are we supposed to do — swim here?"

"We'll come by boat," Griffin replied readily.

Even shy Melissa was galvanized, her beady eyes wide. "Where are we going to get a boat?"

Ben understood all too well. "Oh, no, you don't! Not him! No way!"

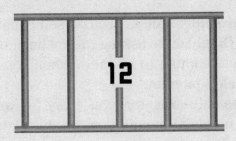

12

Darren Vader wore his Grinch smile — a diabolical grin that stretched from ear to ear. "Really? The Man With The Plan needs me to be part of one of his world-famous operations? What an honor!"

It was Monday, after lunch. Griffin, Ben, and Savannah had followed Darren out of the cafeteria and cornered him at his locker.

Griffin scowled. He had never been a Darren fan and did not relish the idea of involving him in the zoobreak. "You won't be *part* of the operation, just transportation. Like bank robbers need a wheelman to drive the getaway car. Only instead of driving, you'll be sailing."

"A sail man," Ben added.

The smile faded. "You're some piece of work, Bing. You're asking for my help, but I'm not good enough to be there when you boost Drysdale's monkey."

"That's better for you," Griffin argued. "Less involved means less trouble if we get caught."

"Right," the big boy said sarcastically. "All I have to do is sneak out in the middle of the night, steal my dad's boat, and sail you to Rutherford Point so you can break into private property and kidnap a zoo animal."

"Hey," piped up Savannah, "Cleo is rightfully mine."

"That's your opinion, not the cops'. So don't talk to me about being less involved. I'd be involved enough to ask this question —" Darren leaned against the wall, stroking at chin whiskers that were not there. "What's in it for me?"

"We're helping Savannah," Griffin explained.

"That's what's in it for Drysdale. What's in it for *me*? I'll give you a hint — *ka-ching!*"

"You mean money?" Ben asked in amazement. "There's no money."

"Sorry, guys. It'll never work." Darren glanced at the hall clock. "Recess time, already? I think I hear a soccer ball calling my name —" He took a step toward the double doors.

"I'll pay you!" Savannah blurted suddenly.

Darren froze, his Grinch smile reblooming. "Now we're talking. Okay, let's see — a half-day sailboat rental with an experienced captain —"

"Experienced at ripping people off," Ben put in resentfully.

"— plus danger pay — three hundred bucks!"

"Aw, come on!" Griffin exploded. "What kid can get his hands on that kind of money?"

Savannah didn't even blink. This might have been a game to Darren, but she took Cleopatra's future very seriously. "I don't have that much. But I'll give you my allowance for the next three months."

Darren's eyes narrowed. "Six."

"Done."

Griffin pulled a folded piece of paper from his pocket and handed it to Darren. It was a detailed map of the north shore of Long Island, with Cedarville's marina and the Rutherford Point Preserve highlighted. "Commit this route to memory. We don't want to end up in Bermuda."

Savannah pressed her lips together in an expression of hopeful determination. "When are we doing it, Griffin? *All Aboard Animals* moves on at the end of this week."

Griffin held his arms wide, drawing them into his confidence. "Wednesday, after midnight," he announced in a low voice. "Everything will be ready by then."

Wednesday.

Two days away.

When Melissa opened the door of the Dukakis house, Griffin and Ben both checked the number on the door to make sure they'd come to the right address. Her curtain of hair was neatly parted and pinned back, revealing a face that was not all that familiar because it appeared so seldom.

"I made guacamole," she greeted, showing them inside.

"Oh, great," said Griffin, a little perplexed. "Uh — why?"

The question seemed to stump her, so she wheeled out a serving cart with the dip and a basket of chips the size of an eagle's nest.

"You might be hungry?" she suggested finally.

They stood in the front hall, snacking awkwardly.

"This is good," Ben offered lamely. "Spicy."

"I don't have a lot of people over," Melissa admitted. "None, actually. I mean, you guys are the first."

Griffin dusted the crumbs from his fingers. "Now let's check out the webcams."

They trooped up to her small room, which was so cluttered with computers, printers, scanners, and modems that there was barely room for her bed. Four monitors displayed the live feed from the wireless webcams she had planted around the floating zoo.

From watching these, Melissa had been able to put together an *All Aboard Animals* timeline:

6:00 p.m. – closing time

6:10 p.m. – visitors gone, entrance shut

7:30 p.m. – Mr. Nasty leaves for hotel

9:00 p.m. – gangway raised for the night

11:00 p.m. – lights out in Klaus's cabin

"It's perfect," Griffin decided. "We'll meet tomorrow at midnight, and by the time we sail to Rutherford Point, Mr. Nasty will be gone and Klaus will be asleep."

"We hope," added Ben.

"We *know*," Griffin amended. "A good plan leaves nothing to chance. If it happens at *All Aboard Animals*, we see it on these screens."

The words had barely passed his lips when a menacing shape appeared before the interior-view webcam. It grew larger and larger until it completely filled the monitor. For an instant, there was wild, frenzied action, and sharp claws slashed at the camera. Then the screen went dark.

Ben was wide-eyed. "What was *that*?"

Melissa was at the keyboard, typing at light speed. "The video feed has stopped. The camera is offline."

"What do you mean, offline?" Griffin asked.

"Either the camera failed or the transmitter did," she explained. "Maybe the battery died early."

"Or," Ben added uneasily, "our webcam just got eaten by that — that *thing*!"

"There's no thing," Griffin said, a little less certain than he would have liked.

"So what was it, then?"

"How about this: Klaus finds the minicamera. He doesn't know what it is, but it's stuck in a wad of gum, so he chucks it in the trash."

Ben was not convinced. "That didn't look human to me."

Melissa had a theory. "It might have been a ghost image generated by the webcam as it lost power."

"See?" Griffin was triumphant. "Mystery solved."

"I said it *might* have been," she amended. "We can't be sure."

"Well, we definitely have to find out before we get on the boat with it —" Ben regarded his friend with alarm. "Don't we?"

"Zero hour is already set," Griffin argued. "There's no way we can put it off. It's supposed to rain on Thursday, and who knows if Darren can sail in bad weather? And Friday, *All Aboard Animals* moves on. It's now or never."

"So much for 'a good plan leaves nothing to chance,'" Ben complained. "I'd say an unidentified webcam-eating monster counts as leaving something to chance."

Griffin couldn't allow himself to be distracted by his friend's jitters.

The countdown was on.

13

Dressed in a black sweater and his darkest jeans, Griffin sat in his bedroom window, glaring at the tiny square of light coming from the garage door below. What a time for Dad to pull one of his late-night marathons on the Rollo-Bushel! Forty-five minutes to Operation Zoobreak, and he was still in his workshop, tinkering.

Right now, Griffin knew, Ben was tiptoeing out the sliding door at the back of the Slovak home. If he reached the rendezvous spot and Griffin was a no-show, he'd have a heart attack. Loyaltywise, the kid was rock solid, but he had a very low freak-out threshold.

What was that? Griffin heard footsteps on the stairs and peered out the window again. The garage light was off! He heard his father in the bathroom for a few minutes, water splashing in the sink, and the small motor of an electric toothbrush. Then more footsteps and the *whump* of his parents' bedroom door closing.

The hardest part was waiting to make sure Dad was asleep. Minutes passed like weeks. School today had been even worse. Who could concentrate on English or math on the day of an operation? Between periods, he'd rushed to the library to check the online boating forecast. It was always the same: *SE winds 10–15 knots, seas 1–2 ft, light swells.* Griffin didn't even know what a knot was, but he assumed Darren would.

At last, the coast was clear. He threw his backpack over his shoulder and tiptoed down the stairs, wincing at the clinking sound made by the three flashlights and heavy-duty wire cutters inside. As silently as he could, he slipped out the back door, got on his bike, and rode to the small park where he was meeting Ben.

As he approached the rendezvous point, a blinding beam assaulted his eyes.

"What kept you?" Ben demanded, his face white behind his flashlight.

"I'll explain on the way!" Griffin promised.

Eleven jet-propelled minutes later, they pedaled up to the Cedarville Marina at the north end of town. There they found Savannah, Melissa, Logan, and Pitch, waiting not very patiently on the narrow, rocky beach.

"You're late!" Savannah seethed.

"Trouble sneaking out," Griffin explained briskly, taking stock of their faces. "Where's Darren?"

"He's not here yet," Pitch said. She surveyed the line of bobbing watercraft in the nearby slips. "I wonder which boat is the Vaders'."

"Look for the S.S. *Bigmouth*," Ben suggested.

"Don't knock Darren," Savannah said sharply. "Without him, we'd have no way to get to Rutherford Point. If he takes us to Cleo, he can be Sir Bigmouth of the Round Table."

"Okay," said Griffin. "Equipment check."

They ran through the list of gear, piling it up on the sand between them. Everything was ready.

Melissa consulted the clock on her BlackBerry, which was monitoring the three surviving webcams. "It's twelve-twenty-five," she ventured timidly.

"Isn't that just like Darren," Pitch spat. "He helps us, but first he has to make us sweat."

Logan spoke up. "I know some good breathing exercises for stage fright."

Savannah was too wired to be patient. "Let's not and say we did."

Griffin had the last word on the subject. "Calm down, you guys. All we can do is wait."

The zoobreak team paced nervously, the task ahead weighing heavily on their young shoulders. A chill wind came off the water, making them glad they were all in warm sweaters and fleeces. Time ticked away. No Darren.

The BlackBerry told the tale. "One a.m.," Melissa reported blandly.

They all knew, but it took Pitch's plain talk to put it into words: "That backstabbing rat-creep! He stood us up!"

Savannah was devastated. "But what about Cleo?"

"He stood her up, too," Griffin said grimly. "Especially her."

"You mean that's it?" she persisted. "We just go home?"

Griffin tried to make her understand. "Every good plan has built-in options for what you can do when something goes wrong. But there's always a spot where there's no plan B — where it has to happen exactly right or not at all. Getting to Rutherford Point is the linchpin of everything. There's nothing we can do."

Shy Melissa spoke up. "There's one thing we can do." Everyone stared at her. "We can wait longer. Darren probably isn't coming, but maybe he is. It's better than giving up."

The team digested this. There was a strange simplicity to Melissa's thinking that had the ring of the wisdom of the ages.

"You're dreaming," said Pitch. "He's a no-show."

"We'll take a vote," The Man With The Plan decided. "All in favor of going home . . ." Pitch, Logan, and Griffin. "And of staying . . ." Savannah and Melissa. "Home wins, three to two." He froze. "Wait a minute — where's Ben?"

They looked around. Ben was nowhere to be seen.

Out came their flashlights, and they searched the marina. No Ben.

And then Griffin heard a telltale snort — one he had heard many times before. Snoring!

He followed the sound along the beach until his flashlight illuminated Ben, fast asleep, curled up on a pile of fishing nets in an ancient wooden rowboat.

"Ben!" he hissed.

"I'm awake!" the smaller boy exclaimed, scrambling to attention. He took in his surroundings in drowsy embarrassment. "Oh, man, I crashed! Is Darren here yet?"

Griffin didn't answer. His gleaming eyes were focused on two wooden oars lying inside the old dory.

Transportation.

14

Ben dragged the heavy oar through the water, his eyes focused on Griffin, who stood in the dory's bow like Washington crossing the Delaware.

"The preserve was a long ride by bus because we had to drive down one neck and up another," Griffin explained, his flashlight trained on the map in his hands. "By water we can just cut straight across. It can't be more than a mile or two."

"Two miles is pretty far by *rowing*!" Ben panted. "Especially if the boat sinks halfway there."

Pitch examined the wooden deck. "I think she's seaworthy. The floor's totally dry."

"Only because I haven't thrown up yet," wheezed Logan, who was prone to seasickness. "No actor should have to work in these conditions."

"The acting part's over," Griffin told him. "It's all search and rescue from here on in."

Savannah took the oar from Ben's hands. "Here, I'll row for a while. Maybe somebody should give Melissa a break, too."

"That's okay." Even from behind the curtain of hair, Melissa's eyes glowed like a pair of hovering fireflies. "This is really cool."

The eeriest part was when they got far enough from shore that the Cedarville Marina faded into an endless dark coastline. They couldn't see their destination, but home had disappeared, too. It was like being lost at sea.

The journey progressed with agonizing slowness. After one of their flashlights died, Griffin declared a new rule: No more than three lights on at a time to conserve battery power.

"Are we there yet?" groaned Pitch, staring up at the starry sky.

"I think I'm going to start barfing now," Logan gurgled.

"Go ahead," said Savannah. "It's a normal function for all living creatures."

"Just lean over the side," Griffin added. "Remember, this is a round-trip cruise."

Two a.m. found them still in open water. By this time, the simple act of rowing had become backbreakingly painful. The team members took their turns on the oars. Even Melissa grew exhausted and agreed to rest.

She passed her oar off to a none-too-steady Logan and retreated behind her hair. Suddenly, she sat bolt upright, waving her BlackBerry urgently at the others.

"Look!"

Ben squinted at the small screen. It was the portside webcam view. It showed the darkened paddleboat and — far offshore in the distance — three tiny bobbing lights.

"It's us!" Ben exclaimed. "Our flashlights!"

Tired celebration broke out on the dory as the BlackBerry was passed around the team. They had found Rutherford Point.

Savannah began to row with renewed vigor. "Hang in there, Cleo," she murmured determinedly. "I'm coming to get you."

The rowers picked up their pace. Soon, they could identify the lights of the preserve and at last, the gray silhouette of *All*

Aboard Animals growing larger and larger off their bow.

"Oars up!" commanded Griffin in a low voice.

The dory skimmed along the black water until it bumped softly against the heavy steel hull.

Ben gazed at the paddleboat's rail several feet above their heads. "The rope ladder!" he rasped. "Darren was bringing it! Now what are we supposed to do?"

Pitch was already knotting fishing nets together. "Relax." She leaped up and clamped sure hands onto the gunwale of the larger craft. Then she swung her body over the rail onto the deck. A mountaineering knot affixed one end of the nets to an iron cleat. The other she tossed down to Griffin, who secured it to the bow of the dory.

One by one, the team headed up the rat-line formed by the nets and stepped onto the deck. Griffin brought up the rear. From his backpack he produced six pairs of soft cotton surgical booties and passed them around.

"To muffle our footsteps," he explained in a whisper. "We're now in silent mode. Remember — Klaus is on this boat, and we've heard from Logan he's a very light sleeper.

You all know the plan: Ben goes in first, and when he opens the front door, we want to be in and out with the monkey ASAP. The longer it takes, the greater the chance that someone's going to make noise. And we all know what that means."

Pitch swallowed hard. "Let's do it."

Griffin and Ben crept aft toward the vent opening. The lifeboat suitcase was just where they'd left it, and it was easy for Griffin to boost Ben up to the horn-shaped opening.

In his heart of hearts, Ben was half hoping that the four screws holding the vent grating would be too rusted to turn. But the grill came off easily, and the way in yawned wide.

He peered down at his best friend, who was perched on the lifeboat suitcase. "What if I fall asleep in there?"

"You won't," Griffin said. "You already napped back at the marina."

Ben wriggled into the dusty duct, fighting a burning desire to sneeze. He felt like Santa Claus, squeezing through a chimney. Come to think of it, Santa had it easy. He was always welcome. No wonder the old guy was so jolly. He wasn't trying to commit Grand Theft Monkey.

The passage was tight but smooth, so progress was steady. There it was, dead ahead in his flashlight beam — the vent! A measure of relief washed over him. He was actually going to make it. Operation Zoobreak was just beginning, but at least this part — the part he'd been dreading the most — was almost done.

He slithered forward and trained his flashlight straight down into the compartment below. The sight he saw there would give him nightmares for the rest of his life.

Instead of the room with the monkey cage, the beam shone directly into the sleeping face of Klaus Anthony. Even more horrific, the security guard's eyes popped open and stared straight up into the light.

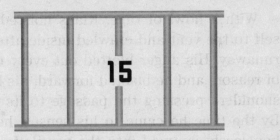

15

Wild with terror, Ben tried to scramble away but only succeeded in whacking his head on the roof of the duct. Dazed, he toppled forward onto the grating. It gave way, and the grill, the flashlight, and Ben dropped right onto Klaus. The cry of shock from the security guard vibrated throughout the entire ship.

Ben took off like Superman, clawing at air and bulkhead — anything to get him up, up, and away. Klaus rose, too, reaching groggily for the intruder. Ben's bootie-clad sneaker came down on the security guard's blond head. It was the boost Ben needed. He was back in the duct, wiggling like a terrified snake in a desperate bid for escape.

With a howl of rage, Klaus hoisted himself to the vent and crawled inside after the runaway. His anger blotted out every ounce of reason, and he blasted forward, his broad shoulders pressing the passage to its limit. By the time he came to his senses, he was hopelessly jammed into the ventilation system — unable to go forward, unable to retreat, his bare feet dangling from the ceiling above his bunk.

With his flashlight lost and the wedged Klaus blocking the way out, Ben was trapped in the narrow duct in utter darkness. The very air reverberated with Klaus's shouting. Of all the worst-case scenarios Ben had imagined, this topped everything — pure, unadulterated horror.

He felt like a blind mouse trapped in a pipe, squirming frantically toward . . . what? It was so dark that he couldn't even see the walls of the duct inches from his face. How was he going to find his way out of here?

He was never going to forgive Griffin for this! Boarding school in New Jersey was a picnic compared to the spot he was in right now.

Klaus was still shouting threats, his booming voice echoing in the metal enclosure.

But wait! A powerful smell reached him. The zoo! He surged forward until his probing hands rattled the grill of another vent opening.

He pounded on the grating until it came loose and clattered to the deck. In his enthusiasm to be free from the ductwork, he very nearly followed it in a swan dive. But he managed to maneuver his legs through the opening so he could drop to the cabin below.

He landed hard and rolled, panting and choking on dust. A familiar animal chattering met his ears.

The dim glow of moonlight through the porthole illuminated the compartment. Ben looked around breathlessly. In the cage bolted to the wall, Cleopatra darted and chirped, unnerved by the chaos. Somehow, he had managed to blunder into exactly the cabin he'd been trying to reach in the first place!

Heart pounding, he barreled through the heart of the zoo, navigating the maze of excited animals awakened by Klaus's bellowing. He threw open the main hatch and burst onto the deck, where he collided with Griffin, nearly bowling him over.

"Ben — you're okay!"

"Cleo!" Savannah made a run for the door, but Ben held her back.

"I'm not okay! None of us are! Klaus is on the loose!" Gulping air, Ben wheezed out the story of how he'd fallen from the ceiling onto the sleeping security guard.

"Wait a minute!" Griffin interrupted. "*Klaus* followed you into the duct?" He put his finger to his lips and listened. The shouts and threats were much less frequent now, replaced by the reverberating sound of pounding against metal.

"He's . . . stuck?" Logan concluded in amazement.

"I barely fit up there myself!" Ben put in breathlessly.

"Let's get Cleo!" exclaimed Savannah.

The sudden presence of six intruders waving flashlights in the dark zoo boat put the animals' agitation level over the top. Furry bodies bounced off the sides of their small enclosures. The hen flapped its wings; the beaver splashed what was left of its water. Feral noises filled the air.

At the sight of Savannah, Cleopatra tried to blast clear through the bars of her cage.

"I'm here, sweetie. Everything's okay . . ." the girl soothed in a flowery tone that bore little resemblance to her urgency the moment before.

While Savannah spoke, Griffin went to work on the cage with the wire cutters. He squeezed with all his might, but the metal resisted. An instant of panic — had they gone through all this only to fail at freeing the monkey?

There was a snap as the bar gave way. Relieved, he cut through the others until Savannah could draw her beloved capuchin out of the enclosure into an ecstatic embrace.

Yet even in this joyful reunion, Cleopatra did not calm down. The furry head jerked around relentlessly, scanning the exhibit for some unseen danger.

Savannah was mystified. "I thought she'd be okay once we sprang her, but she's even more rattled than before."

"Maybe she's freaked out by all the yelling," Pitch suggested.

Savannah shook her head. "I think she's trying to tell me something."

An otherworldly screech cut the air.

16

A murky shadow swooped down on Cleopatra. Terrified, the monkey buried her face in Savannah's chest. In a flash of sharp claws, the attacker swiped at the capuchin's back, not missing by much. The team felt rather than saw two powerful wing beats as the creature disappeared into the blackness.

"What was that?" breathed Logan in awe.

To Ben, the incident was all too familiar. "The monster that ate Melissa's webcam!"

Flashlight beams panned the compartment from top to bottom.

"Where did it go?" squeaked Melissa.

"Who cares?" Pitch was impatient. "We've got Cleo. Let's blow this Popsicle stand!"

"Not yet," said Savannah in an angry tone. "I've got a feeling about this 'monster.'"

She marched into the exhibit's main compartment and shone her torch on the owl cage. It was empty, the door wide.

"That jerk, Mr. Nasty," she seethed. "That low-down, animal-abusing criminal. As if it wasn't bad enough that he runs his zoo like a prison — he turns the owl loose at night to terrorize the poor little creatures so they'll be too scared to try to get out of their cages!" Her voice rose in volume until she was drowning out the cries of Klaus in the ductwork.

"All the more proof that we're doing the right thing," Griffin decided. "Luckily, we had the perfect plan."

"Perfect?" Pitch exploded. "Darren never showed! Ben practically died tonight! There's a guy trapped in the ceiling! And now we've got to row a million miles on the world's slowest boat and pray we can find Cedarville again!"

"There were a couple of hiccups," Griffin admitted. "But now we're in good shape. Keep hold of Cleo and let's get out of here before Hoo over there comes back for another dive-bombing run."

"We can't," Savannah said.

Griffin was taken aback. "What are you

talking about? This whole operation is for *you* — to save your monkey!"

"And I'm grateful," she told him. "But if we take Cleo and go, we'll be leaving all these other animals in the hands of a cruel man who mistreats them. We have to rescue everybody."

The protests bubbled up from all sides:

"Are you nuts?"

"There are too many of them!"

"We need a bigger boat!"

"Like Noah's Ark!"

"It's not part of the plan," Griffin concluded.

Savannah was adamant. "I don't care about the plan. If it's right for Cleo, it's right for the whole zoo."

"No, it isn't," Ben argued. "The monkey is yours. But you don't own the chipmunks and the beaver and the ferret. And you definitely don't own that bloodthirsty raptor!"

"We're all members of the animal kingdom. We have to stand up for our brothers and sisters."

Behind them, the piglet oinked in agreement.

Griffin sighed. "Look, Savannah. I know this must be hard. But it won't work."

Still hugging Cleopatra, Savannah sat down on a stool. "You guys go. Cleo and I are staying."

"Don't be stupid," Griffin snapped. "You'll get caught."

"That's what I want. If I can't rescue everybody, the next best thing is to get arrested. Then there will be so much publicity that this so-called zoo will be exposed as the chamber of horrors that it is."

Pitch blew her stack. "You're crazy! And the worst part is we're going to have to do it just to keep you out of jail!"

Melissa's eyes emerged from her curtain of hair. "It's possible, you know," she said softly. "They're just little animals. There aren't any elephants."

"Even if we *could* get them all out of here, what would we do with them?" Griffin challenged Savannah. "Even you can't have fifty pets."

"Maybe we should set them free," Logan suggested. "Then we'd just have to cut them out of their cages and open the door."

Savannah was horrified. "Absolutely not!

Mr. Nasty trained that owl to attack! Half of them won't make it thirty feet from the boat."

"But isn't that the whole nature thing?" Ben asked. "Survival of the fittest?"

She shook her head. "Not for animals living in captivity. These poor little guys don't have the tools to compete in the wild. We have to take them with us."

"And keep them where?" Griffin demanded.

"In the shed in my backyard," Savannah replied readily. "It'll only be for one night. First thing tomorrow, I'll call Dr. Alford. She finds places for animals all the time."

"That'll be an interesting conversation," Pitch predicted. "'Oh, hi. I knocked off a zoo boat last night, so my shed's full of critters. What's new with you?'"

"Dr. Alford doesn't judge. She just wants what's best for the animals. And she has contacts at every zoo and wildlife preserve in the country. I know she'll help."

Griffin heaved a sigh of resignation. "Fine, we'll take them all. But we're going to have to get Hoo under control before we crack open these cages."

"Can I make a suggestion?" Pitch flicked the switch on the bulkhead, and the lights came on in the exhibit.

Even Cleopatra shielded her eyes against the harsh fluorescent glare. A chorus of complaint rose from the animals. The owl's cry was the most angry of all. Hoo flew in erratic circles above their heads, hooting anxiously.

The disturbance even reached the ears of the paddleboat's forgotten inhabitant. "Hey!" Klaus's muffled voice rumbled through the ventilation system. "What's going on down there?"

The team exchanged uneasy glances. They had no great love for the security guard, but no one had anticipated leaving him in such a tight situation.

Logan felt especially guilty. "Klaus?" he called into a grating. "We're going to phone somebody to get you out. Just as soon as we — uh — finish."

There was a long pause. Then: "Ferris? Is that you?"

"Just relax," Logan soothed. "The sooner we load up these animals, the sooner we can send help."

A cry of outrage erupted from the vent, followed by more struggling and banging.

The roundup began. They chased Hoo all through the boat in a series of collisions and near misses until Savannah tossed a tarpaulin over the swooping owl. Grateful for the return of darkness, Hoo allowed himself to be captured. Griffin got busy with the wire cutters, snipping through bars and opening cages. A large cardboard carton became home to the meerkat, prairie dog, chipmunks, squirrels, and beaver. The chicken and piglet were swaddled in Melissa's hoodie. A battered suitcase with a broken fastener became the reptile room, housing the frogs, turtles, salamanders, garter snakes, and chuckwalla. The rabbits fit in an old shopping bag, but the ferret could not be trusted with them, so Ben had to stick it inside his sweater. The duck and the loon fought and had to be stashed in separate boxes. And the hamsters, gerbils, and mice were spread out among everybody's pockets.

"When we get to the boat, we can wrap them in the fishing nets," Savannah told the others. "That'll be more secure."

They carried the whole menagerie outside and moved around the outer deck to starboard, where they had moored the rowboat.

Pitch drew in a deep breath. "Fresh air! I've got to admit — I never thought we'd make it this far!"

They reached the starboard gunwale and peered over the rail. The ratline of fishing nets hung loosely down, stirring with the movement of the waves.

The dory was gone.

17

"Where's the boat?" Logan wailed.

Savannah was mystified. "Did it sink?"

Pitch shook her head. "Then it would still be bobbing at the end of the net." She wheeled on Griffin, furious. "Some *idiot* tied up the boat with a knot he learned in Balloon Animals 101!"

In a frenzy, Griffin panned his flashlight over the surrounding waters.

"What's the point?" groaned Ben. "Even if you spot it, we can't swim for it. Face it, Griffin, we're so dead that even dead people would be amazed how dead we are."

"Not yet!" Griffin exclaimed, stuffing an errant gerbil back in his pocket.

"Give it up!" Pitch snapped. "Even The Man With The Plan can't make a boat out of no boat!"

Griffin ran to the stern and returned dragging the bright yellow suitcase he'd used as a stepstool while boosting Ben up to the vent. "Stand back, everybody!" he cried, pulling the cord.

There was an explosion of compressed gas, and the suitcase began to grow and unfold, morphing into a giant life raft, complete with outboard motor and sun canopy.

Pitch goggled. "I take it all back. You *can* make a boat out of no boat!"

The cruise back to Cedarville was a lot faster than the first trip, mostly because of the life raft's outboard. In fact, in many ways the craft was ideal for a zoobreak. It was meant for a shipwreck and was stocked with food, water, a compass, rain gear, and medical supplies. None of this was of great importance to the team, except that all the gear came in dozens of pouches, packets, and containers. These turned out to be just the right size for stashing small furry animals, some of whom seemed determined to wriggle overboard and/or eat their fellow travelers.

Griffin manned the rudder, his eyes darting from the map to the compass to the approaching coastline. All things considered, he was pretty pleased with the way the operation had worked out. True, there had been a few unexpected twists. But a truly great plan was always able to adapt. And the end result — the rescue of Cleopatra — was a total success. The forty hitchhikers were Savannah's problem — and her friend Dr. Alford's.

Beside him, Melissa worked at her Black-Berry, e-mailing the police department of Rutherford Point to rescue Klaus from the zoo boat ceiling. She knew a way to send the message via a dummy server in Hong Kong. That way, it could never be traced to her.

Pitch was the first to spot the lights of the Cedarville Marina. "When we get off this raft," she vowed, "I'm going to drop to my knees and kiss the ground."

"You guys were fantastic tonight," said Savannah, her voice quavering with emotion. "I'll never forget this."

"Me, neither," Ben assured her. "If I ever get on TV and they ask, 'What's the worst thing that ever happened to you?' this is going to be it."

The shore gradually grew more distinct, and the moored boats loomed out of the darkness. At last, Griffin cut the engine, and the raft ran aground on the beach. The time was 3:35 a.m.

"I see Darren isn't here yet," said Pitch sarcastically, stepping out onto the sand.

Now all that remained was to unload the animals in their pouches and boxes and bike them over to Savannah's shed.

"What about the boat?" Melissa asked, frowning. "If it's found in Cedarville, Mr. Nasty might be able to connect it to us."

Once again, The Man With The Plan had an answer. Together, the team engaged the engine, turned the raft around, and sent it putt-putting toward distant Connecticut.

The bicycle parade started slowly, its riders overburdened by the former inhabitants of the floating zoo. Savannah was in the lead, with Cleopatra sitting piggyback and the tarpaulin containing Hoo in the front basket.

It seemed grossly unfair that this final effort was required of them after all they'd endured tonight. Perhaps a team pushing to the summit of Mount Everest would be more exhausted, but it seemed unlikely.

They rode in silence to avoid waking anyone in the sleeping town. Discovery was unthinkable. Not so close to the finish line.

When they turned the corner and the Drysdale house came into view, a cry of recognition escaped Cleopatra.

"Sweetie — shhh," Savannah said, hushing her.

The sound reached no human ears, but that didn't mean it reached no ears at all. A large, dark shape sailed through an open first-floor window and hit the ground at a full gallop. Luthor closed the gap in seconds, his meaty paws barely touching the pavement. The leap began ten feet away.

Ecstatic, Cleopatra vaulted over Savannah's shoulder and met her best friend in midair.

Savannah dived off her bike just in time. The wipeout was spectacular. She hit the grass and rolled as the bike careened wildly, steering itself into a telephone pole. The collision bounced the tarp out of the basket and sent it spinning and unwrapping along the road.

With a hoot that shattered the quiet of the wee hours, a bundle of brown feathers shot out of the basket like a Tomahawk missile. Hoo circled once and then soared off, vanishing into the night.

Five pairs of eyes stared at Savannah, waiting for her reaction.

She waved, a blissful expression on her face. "He's free," she announced happily.

"I thought animals from captivity can't compete in the wild," Ben reminded her.

"He's the only one who can," she said serenely. "He'll be fine. And all the others will be, too — starting tomorrow."

A contented Cleopatra climbed aboard Luthor for the short trot home.

Hoo circled high above them, exploring this strange new world.

18

The music room faded around Griffin, and the trombone slipped from his nerveless fingers. His head slid backward into the bell of the tuba behind him. The tuba player, Darren Vader, delivered a blast that knocked Griffin out of his chair and into the clarinet section on the riser below.

It didn't sound much like the theme from *Rocky*, but at least it woke him up.

"Griffin Bing!" Mr. Hoberman, the bandleader, exclaimed in exasperation. "Could I trouble you to stay awake?"

It was morning, a few hours after they'd returned, and Operation Zoobreak was taking its toll on Griffin. He believed in planning 100 percent. But no plan could ever account for going to school on eighty-three minutes of sleep.

"Sorry," he mumbled, retrieving his instrument. "It won't happen again." Now he knew how Ben felt when the irresistible sleepiness stole over him — stunned and helpless.

The bandleader sighed. "Go to the boys' room and splash some water on your face. And don't come back until you're ready to be a part of this orchestra."

"Late night, Bing?" Darren snickered behind him.

"No," Griffin hissed. "We had to call it off because some *traitor* didn't show!"

Darren reddened. "I *told* you — my uncle came over, and the guy wouldn't leave! I couldn't get out of the house."

"Sure, sure," Griffin muttered, setting the trombone on its stand and staggering toward the door. He'd already warned the zoobreak team not to tell Darren anything. He couldn't be trusted to keep his big mouth shut any more than he could be trusted to follow through on a promise.

The blast of Darren's tuba still ringing in his ears, Griffin headed for the boys' room. He never got there. The door to the girls' room was flung open, and a small arm reached out and pulled him inside. There stood Savannah, her face white, her eyes wild.

"What's the big idea?" Griffin complained. "If I get caught in here —"

"That's the least of our problems!" Savannah shrilled. She punched a number into a small cell phone and held it to his ear. It rang once before going straight to voicemail:

"You've reached Dr. Kathleen Alford, Curator for the Long Island Zoo. I'm presently in equatorial Africa, supervising the transport of three rain-forest baboons to the United States. I'll be back in the office on Wednesday, April twenty-second. Please leave a message at the tone."

There was a beep, followed by a different voice: "Mailbox full."

In an instant, Griffin's complexion matched Savannah's. "April twenty-second — that's two weeks away! You're going to have to find another zoo!"

"I don't know anybody else who works in a zoo!" Savannah wailed. "Dr. Alford's the only person who could find homes for all those animals!"

"Well, I hope they've got an Internet café at Baboons 'R' Us, because we need her *now*!

What's she doing there for so long, anyway? How hard can it be to mail a baboon to Long Island?"

They heard the squeak of a heavy door and Savannah whispered urgently, "Hide!"

Griffin locked himself into a stall and stood up on the toilet seat to keep his shoes out of view.

Savannah commenced washing her hands. "Hi, Monica."

"Guess what was on the news this morning!" The newcomer was agog. "Remember that zoo boat from the field trip? Somebody broke in last night and stole all the animals!"

Griffin very nearly fell into the toilet.

"Wow," Savannah managed faintly. "That's unbelievable."

"Totally!" Monica agreed. "The crooks loaded all the animals onto a lifeboat and took them to Connecticut! You know what beats me? Why they'd even bother. That was the lousiest zoo in the world."

As soon as Monica was gone, Griffin emerged, looking even paler than before.

"You see, Griffin?" Savannah's agitation was rising. "We're in trouble — and the one person who can save us is out of the country!"

"They think we went to Connecticut," Griffin reflected hopefully.

"They won't think it for long if all the missing animals turn up in Cedarville," Savannah persisted. "You've got to help me!"

"You asked for help last time," he reminded her. "And I came up with a great plan to get your monkey back. Everything would have been fine if we'd just stuck to that. But no. One animal wasn't enough. We had to take forty!"

Savannah was stubborn. "We did the right thing. Those animals are better off in my shed than under Mr. Nasty's thumb."

"For two weeks?" Griffin challenged.

Even Savannah had no answer for that. "No, not for two weeks. It wouldn't be safe, it wouldn't be sanitary, and I definitely couldn't keep it a secret from my parents. Especially not if my dad ever wants to cut the grass."

Griffin ran nervous fingers through his unruly hair. "Okay, let me think."

His mind raced. A big operation always seemed impossible until you broke it down into its many parts. Taken one by one, if all those tiny parts were possible, then the whole plan had to be possible, too.

Maybe that was the approach he needed here. He could never wrap his mind around hiding forty animals. But could they hide *one* animal — and then do it thirty-nine more times?

Aloud, he said, "Logan's house has a leaky basement. That sounds like a pretty good place for a beaver to hang out for a couple of weeks. . . ."

19

The GUEST LIST:

> Kellerman Underground Wetlands – beaver, frogs, salamanders, turtles

> Dukakis Split-Level Prairie – hen, piglet, prairie dog

> Benson Temperate Forest – garter snakes, chipmunks, squirrels

> Drysdale Custom Habitat – capuchin monkey, rabbits, white rats, duck, loon

> Slovak Suburban Desert – chuckwalla, ferret

> Bing Rodent House – hamsters, gerbils, mice, meerkat

"Meerkats are *not* rodents," Savannah lectured at the emergency meeting. "They're actually related to the mongoose family."

"Yeah, well, now we know who to call if there's a cobra infestation," Ben lamented. "I can't believe there's another operation. It isn't even a whole day since the *last* operation. I went from zoobreaker to zookeeper in just a few hours."

The team was gathered in Savannah's yard after school that day for the beginning of Operation Houseguest. Melissa had the wagon she used to deliver the weekly *Pennysaver*. This would serve as transport to distribute the fugitive animals to their temporary safe houses. Luckily, it had been raining off and on all day, so no one in Cedarville would question Melissa's use of the cart's waterproof covering.

"It's only for a couple of weeks," Griffin told the grumbling team. "It'll fly by."

"Yeah, like the Cretaceous period," Ben muttered.

"I know it's a lot to ask," Savannah admitted, "but look at the results of what we've done already." She indicated her huge dog, Luthor, who was carrying Cleopatra on the back of his neck again. If a pair of animals ever looked drenched in joy and contentment, it was those two.

Ben was nervous. "Aren't you afraid that your folks will get suspicious about Cleopatra turning up today of all days?"

Savannah shook her head. "It makes perfect sense. Cleo got loose in the breakout and made her way home. Most animals have an excellent homing instinct."

Pitch ran onto the scene. "Sorry I'm late, you guys. I was glued to the TV. *All Aboard Animals* made CNN."

"But they still think the crooks went to Connecticut, right?" Griffin asked breathlessly.

She nodded. "That's the good news. The bad news is the cops have figured out the zoobreak was done by kids."

"How could they know that?" Savannah demanded.

"Klaus told them," Pitch replied. "They had to free him from the ceiling with the Jaws of Life, that thing they use to cut people out of car wrecks. They've even got a prime suspect — Ferris Atwater, Jr."

Logan was disgusted. "Wouldn't you know

it! I've spent my whole life trying to get on TV, and now I am, but nobody knows it's me! How can I put something like this in a press packet?"

"Maybe they'll print up wanted posters," Ben suggested sarcastically.

"Exactly how much trouble *are* we in?" asked Melissa, the practical one.

"Absolutely none," Griffin assured her, "so long as we don't get caught."

"And if we do?" asked Logan.

"Use your imagination," Pitch suggested sourly. "The cattle rustlers stole animals, too, and they got strung up from the nearest tree."

There was a sober silence as this sunk in. Savannah ended it by opening the door of the shed with a metallic click.

A furry blur jumped from the webbing of a lacrosse stick. It struck Ben full in the chest and clung there, claws gripping the fabric of his sweatshirt.

"Get it off! Get it off!"

"It's just the ferret," Savannah soothed. "Look — he likes you."

"No, he doesn't! He's clawing me to death!"

"Ferrets are carnivores," Savannah lectured. "If he wanted to claw you or bite you, he'd at least break the skin. In a high-stress situation, with all these people around, a very young juvenile felt comfortable coming to you. That's genuine affection and trust."

"Besides," Griffin added, consulting the Operation Houseguest plan, "he's on your list. Him and — let's see — the chuckwalla."

Ben was genuinely dismayed. "What's a chuckwalla?"

"A small desert lizard," Savannah explained. "You have the only house with a sauna, so it has to go to you. They do best in hot, dry air."

She reached into the shed, pulled out a fluorescent yellow pouch that had once held signal flares from the life raft, and unzipped it slightly. "Rise and shine, you guys." To the others, she reported, "The mice are hungry."

Griffin checked the paper. "They're coming home with me. What do they eat?"

"Rodent chow," Savannah replied, re-zipping the pack and placing it in Melissa's cart. "In block or pellet form. Your choice."

"They're getting cheese," Griffin decided. "If it works on *Tom and Jerry*, it'll work in my room."

"And plenty of water," Savannah added. "That goes for all the animals. But don't feed them until you place them in their new surroundings. Getting food will make them feel at home so they'll be less likely to try to run away."

The first stop was Logan's house. They lowered the reptile suitcase, minus the garter snakes, in through a basement window, and then dropped the beaver in loose. Everyone heard the splashes.

"How much water do you have down there?" Griffin asked in amazement.

Logan shrugged. "Depends on how rainy it's been. Lucky for us we did the zoobreak before they installed our new sump pump."

"Aren't you worried that your mom is going to go down there?" Pitch wondered.

"Not a chance," Logan scoffed. "There are spiders the size of Mini Coopers in that basement. She's got towels stuffed under the door to make sure they can't come up into the house."

"Spiders — great," Savannah enthused. "That'll take care of the food needs of the frogs and salamanders."

"Don't worry," Logan promised. "This is the safest place in town." And he went into the house to see about making his new boarders comfortable.

Melissa's parents weren't home, so it was simple enough to carry the hen, piglet, and prairie dog up to her bedroom closet. Pitch, who had a full house with two older siblings, had to climb the drainpipe to smuggle the squirrels, chipmunks, and garter snakes inside. Ben kept the ferret in his shirt and the chuckwalla in his jacket pocket and walked straight past his parents at the kitchen counter.

The Drysdale house was so filled with animals anyway that no one was going to notice the three extra rabbits in Savannah's warren, or the two white rats in one of the many pet carriers stacked in the garage. The duck and the loon she finessed into the waterfowl pond in the public park next door.

Griffin's house was the last stop. As he established the four mice, three hamsters, and three gerbils in the sturdy plastic chest of drawers that contained his lifetime supply of Lego, the meerkat peered down at him from its perch on the dresser.

"Just sit tight," he told it.

Sitting tight turned out to be one of its strengths. It didn't budge, following Griffin's every move with dark-rimmed eyes.

As he closed the rodents into their hiding place, promising to return with dinner, he felt a wave of emotion that was almost as strong as his fatigue. Operation Houseguest had sapped his very last ounce of strength. He had nothing left to give to this plan.

But *was* it a real plan? It had been hatched in two seconds in the girls' bathroom at school. There had been no time to think it through, refine it, or pay attention to the details.

Yes, they had gotten the animals safely hidden before anyone noticed the menagerie in the Drysdales' shed. But there were so many things that could go wrong. It would only take one escaped meerkat, or prairie dog, or chuckwalla for the authorities to stop looking in Connecticut and start looking here. He remembered from the baseball card heist that cops were very good at their jobs. It would be impossible to cover the tracks of forty animals if the police were nosing around. And then who knew how much trouble they'd be in? Mr. Nasty didn't look like the forgiving type. And as for Klaus . . .

He wished he could feel more in control. Like he was running the plan instead of the other way around.

Get a grip!

Well, the first way to do that was to find a good spot for the meerkat.

Out the window, the sun glinted off the glass panes of his mother's small backyard greenhouse. It was a makeshift affair — a rectangular foundation of cinder blocks for the walls, with an old window resting on top. But it was warm, roomy, subtropical — and best of all, Mom only used it in March to get a head start on her flower garden. This place had meerkat written all over it.

Mom was out, and Dad was in the garage, working on the Rollo-Bushel. So Griffin hustled the little animal out to the yard and stuffed him under the glass of the greenhouse. It was twenty degrees warmer in there, and the meerkat perked up immediately.

Savannah had told him all about the meerkat diet, but he'd forgotten every word of it.

So he brought a bowl of water and a handful of Ritz crackers.

The meerkat chowed down happily, and Griffin, encouraged, had a couple of crackers himself.

Maybe a plan didn't have to be flawless to have a chance of working.

20

Ben was sleeping so deeply, so soundly, that when the nip came, it was like being shot from a cannon through six levels of dreamscape into harsh reality.

"Ow! Cut it out, Mom!"

It wasn't Mom. When his eyes focused, he was staring into the snout of a huge, ravening beast with a slavering mouth full of jagged, razor-sharp teeth. At the last second, he managed to swallow the cry of terror that surely would have brought his parents — and everybody within a three-block radius — running.

It was the ferret, poised on his chest, propping itself up on two tiny front paws that pushed against Ben's chin. The feral eyes peered anxiously down at him.

Shocked, Ben jumped up, sending the animal flying. It landed in mid-scurry and disappeared under the bed.

There was a knock at the door and Mr. Slovak poked his head inside. "Time to get up for school," he called.

"Thanks, Dad," Ben replied, then added, "You don't have to wake me anymore. I'll use my clock radio from now on."

"Sure, Ben. I'm glad to see you taking responsibility. This kind of independence is really going to help you at the academy."

His father's comment brought him up short. The academy. It was a reminder that there were worse things than having a ferret under your bed.

He dressed quickly and ran down to breakfast, careful to close his bedroom door behind him. En route to the kitchen, he made a detour to the basement, where the sauna was located next to the Jacuzzi. The chuckwalla looked all right, he supposed, stretched out on the bench close to the coals. How could you tell if a lizard wasn't doing well? Would it get pale? What color is pale when you're already gray?

And what was that on the bench? BBs?

He stared in horror. *Poop! It pooped in our sauna!*

He picked up the droppings with a tissue and flushed them, trying to keep his mind in neutral. Then he turned on the heat, twisting the timer all the way to the maximum.

"You've got thirty minutes of desert," he whispered. "After that, you've got to chill out till I get home from school."

At breakfast, he was positive his parents would be able to read the guilt on his face. But they seemed not to notice how stressed he was. He hoped neither of them was looking forward to a nice relaxing sauna in the next two weeks.

Back in his room, he found the ferret up on the bed again. From his pocket he produced a napkin-wrapped sausage patty smuggled off the breakfast table.

Ferrets are carnivores, Savannah had said. She was right. The patty was devoured eagerly.

"Now we just have to find someplace to put you while I'm at school," Ben mused aloud. He was pleasantly surprised that the creature allowed itself to be picked up. "Good ferret," he approved.

He opened his sock drawer and dropped his roommate inside. But before he could shut it again, the ferret sprang back onto his arm.

He tried it three more times with the identical result. On the third effort, the animal crawled down his collar and buried itself under his shirt.

"Ben —" came a call from the front hall. "You're going to be late."

He looked down his shirt to see the black eyes staring stubbornly up at him.

"All right, Ferret Face, looks like you're coming with me."

Griffin met Ben at the halfway point of their walk to school. The two friends were exhaustion twins. Each could see his own dark circles around the other's eyes.

"How's it going?" Griffin asked, even though he wasn't sure he wanted to hear the answer.

Ben bristled. "I've got a chuckwalla in my sauna and a ferret in my shirt. How do you think it's going?"

"In your shirt? You mean *now*?" He scrutinized Ben's upper body. "That wasn't part of the plan! What if a teacher sees him?"

"He wouldn't let me leave without him," Ben explained. "Maybe Savannah's right. He likes me."

"Just be careful," Griffin urged. "We've already had one close call. Pitch's mom almost found the garter snakes in the French-press coffeemaker."

Ben shook his head miserably. "I wish there was some way we could click our heels together, blink three times, and fast forward two weeks to when the zoo lady will be here to take these lousy animals off our hands."

At school, the buzz of conversation was all about the mass breakout at the floating zoo. Mr. Nastase had already appeared on several local morning shows, pretending to care about the safety of his former exhibits.

Savannah was outraged. "Can you believe that criminal? He was crying on the interviewer! Sobbing! That jerk never looked away from his cash box long enough to notice his animals until they were gone!"

"You can't blame people for being interested," Pitch put in. "Every science and biology class took a field trip to Rutherford Point for that exhibit. That's half the school. And the fact that the suspects are kids, too, only makes it juicier. The way people talk about Ferris Atwater, Jr., he's like a folk hero — a cross between Robin Hood and Doctor Dolittle."

"I hate him," Logan said bitterly. "How come he gets to be famous, and I get cut out of a stupid orange juice commercial?"

"You can't hate him," Melissa pointed out. "He's you."

"Never mind Ferris Atwater, Jr.," Savannah interrupted. "How are the animals doing? How's the beaver?"

"It's not as much of a no-brainer as I thought it was going to be," Logan admitted. "Every time I go down to feed the turtles, he slaps the water with his tail. It's scaring the salamanders."

"At least a beaver doesn't cluck," put in Melissa, hostess to the chicken.

"Or scurry," added Pitch, who was in charge of the squirrel and chipmunk contingent.

Ben was not to be outdone. "You've got troubles with your animals. Big deal. I have a *relationship* with mine." He flipped up his shirt and gave everyone a quick peek at Ferret Face, clinging to the cotton weave. "Lucky me."

Melissa shook her curtain of hair aside and peered at them earnestly. "I don't want to make things worse, but my dad was talking about an incident that was reported to the town last night. Some lady's Chihuahua got ambushed from the air and barely escaped in one piece. Based on the description, they're pretty sure the attacker was an owl."

"Hoo!" Ben rasped.

"Forget that," Pitch exclaimed, annoyed. "We have enough hassles with the animals we've got. We shouldn't have to worry about the one that got away."

"Except," Griffin reasoned, "if the cops put two and two together and realize that owl and Mr. Nasty's owl are the same owl —"

"What owl?" Darren Vader joined the group. Everyone took one step away from contact with him.

"I didn't say owl; I said *towel*," Griffin shot back. "The one I cleaned the sewer with and then rubbed on your toothbrush."

If Darren was offended, he didn't let on. "Funny thing — an owl is one of the animals that got stolen off the paddleboat. But, hey, you wouldn't know anything about that."

"Right," Savannah said threateningly. "We don't."

"That's a crazy coincidence," Darren went on. "You guys plan a zoobreak and then another group of kids does exactly the same thing on the same night."

"Truth is stranger than fiction," Pitch said through clenched teeth.

"You know who'd find this whole thing really fascinating?" Darren persisted. "The cops. They love coincidences."

The team exchanged uneasy glances.

Griffin spoke up first. "If you have a point, make it and go away."

"I want a piece of the action," Darren replied readily.

"Action?" Ben repeated. "What action?"

"Don't play dumb with me," Darren growled. "Those animals are worth money. Some of them are probably worth a lot of money."

That pushed all Savannah's buttons. "You can't put a price tag on an animal's life!" she raged. "You're talking about forty beating hearts!"

Darren grinned triumphantly. "I'll take that as a confession."

Griffin juggled his anger and the need to choose his words carefully. "If we had them — which we don't — and we sold them — which we won't — we wouldn't give one red cent to the traitor who stabbed us in the back when he was supposed to help us go get them — which we didn't."

The bell rang, and the students around them began heading for homeroom.

"Anyway, think it over," Darren said in a friendly tone. "Oh, by the way, I read a description of this kid Ferris Atwater, Jr. Kind of reminds me of you, Kellerman."

It was a tense start to what promised to be a tense day. The team knew from past experience that Darren was a bad enemy.

Logan alone wore a smile as the group broke up. He was finally famous — even if it was only to Darren Vader.

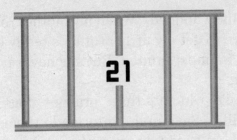

21

Griffin opened the toy chest and peered inside. "Amazing," he said. "I wouldn't have believed it if I wasn't seeing it with my own eyes."

About a dozen stuffed animals were piled in the cedar chest. Among them, completely motionless, sat the prairie dog, one hundred percent real, blending in so well that it was impossible to tell it from the toys.

Melissa nodded. "When my mother reached in there to get my little brother's teddy bear, I swear I almost fainted. But she never noticed a thing."

"You're lucky that prairie dogs stay so still," Savannah informed them. She looked approvingly into the closet, which was lined with ripped-up newspapers. "Dried corn, seeds, plenty of water — that's fine for the hen. What are you feeding the piglet?"

"Leftovers," Melissa replied. "He's like a little pink garbage disposal. He had General Tso's chicken last night. The only problem is I'm going through a lot of newspaper."

"The Sunday *Times* comes tomorrow," Griffin put in helpfully.

"You're doing great," Savannah approved. "Only —" She looked around. "Where's the mud?"

Melissa's beady eyes were wide open now. "Mud?"

"It keeps their skin hydrated," Savannah explained.

"This is a house, not a pigsty," Melissa complained. She was anxious to please her friends, but come on! "There's no mud."

Savannah was adamant. "If you can't bring

the mud to the pig, you have to bring the pig to the mud."

"No way," Griffin jumped in. "That's a security risk. Too easy to get caught carrying him in and out."

"Hang on a sec." Savannah stepped into the bathroom in the hall. She returned a moment later with a large tube filled with a viscous gray cream. "This should do the trick."

Melissa was horrified. "That's my mother's imported Sumatran volcanic mud pack. It costs forty dollars a tube!"

Savannah nodded understandingly. "Better use it only once a day."

> 10:33 a.m. - BENSON HOUSE GARAGE

Pitch was plainly worried. "The squirrels can still drink a little water, but the chipmunks have stopped eating altogether."

Savannah reached into the picnic basket that served as the chipmunk house and retrieved a striped ball of fluff. "What are you feeding them?"

"Peanut butter, extra crunchy."

Savannah's eyes widened. "Why?"

"You said they eat nuts. That's the closest thing we have."

"Look at the poor little sweeties! You've glued their mouths shut! Quick — a toothbrush!"

"No way!"

Savannah sighed. "A Q-tip, then. Hurry!"

Griffin shook his head. This was not a good sign.

> 11:09 a.m. – DUCK POND IN PARK NEXT TO DRYSDALE HOUSE

"Hey, Mommy," the little boy announced worriedly. "That duck is sick!"

He was pointing at the loon, which had just sent out its distinctive warbling call in the midst of a whole lot of quacking.

"I hear stuff like that through my window about ten times a day," Savannah said wearily. "Face it, Griffin. The loon's too different." It was undeniable. The bird had dark, almost black feathers, a ruff around its neck, and a narrow, pointy beak. "It's smaller than the others, except maybe the teals. And it's a diver. People are talking about it way too much."

"Maybe we should sneak it out tonight," Griffin suggested. "It can go into Logan's basement."

"Don't be stupid. It would eat the frogs and salamanders. And the noise! I mean, it's not bad here — outside. But a damp basement is like an echo chamber!"

Griffin shook his head. "I was nervous about the rest of us. The one person I was sure would ace Operation Houseguest was you."

Savannah laughed without humor. "Are you kidding? My own rabbits can't stand the new rabbits, and it's World War Three in the warren. You can know everything about zoology, but no one can predict a personality conflict."

Griffin checked his watch. "We should probably head over to Ben's. He's ordering pizza for lunch. Ferret Face likes pepperoni. Then we can go to Logan's."

> 1:12 p.m. - KELLERMANS' BASEMENT

The scene was something out of a dream. All the parts were normal enough, but they didn't fit together logically. The floor was covered in at least six inches of water, and a beaver swam in circles around an island formed by a sodden beanbag chair. Turtles and salamanders lived on this island, joined by frogs, which splashed in and out of the water at will.

"It's amazing!" Savannah breathed. "It's like a whole ecosystem sprang up in somebody's leaky basement!"

"It's starting to creep me out a little," Logan confessed. "See those bookshelves over there? They're all chewed up. I think the beaver's eating them."

"He's definitely got the teeth for it," Griffin observed lamely.

"No, that's not it at all!" Savannah pointed to a small mound of debris poking up from the water near the stairs. "He's building a dam! Logan, this is wonderful! You've created a habitat so perfect that he's actually doing what normal beavers do!"

Logan looked miserable. "You wouldn't think it was so wonderful if it was *your* basement. When they pump this place out, someone's going to have to explain why there's a beaver dam down here!" He turned beseeching eyes on The Man With The Plan. "I can't go on like this for two weeks! You've got to find a way to end it!"

He was almost in tears, and not acting this time. Not even a little bit.

"I suggest using toothpicks to remove the rodent droppings from your Lego drawers," Savannah was saying. "Otherwise, you're going to have an odor problem."

Griffin was preoccupied. "Do you think Logan's right? That we're crazy to try to keep this going for two weeks?"

"We just have to take it one day at a time," Savannah replied, "and do our best for the animals."

"I'm worried about Ben. His dark circles are getting bigger. That ferret is waking him up when he —" He hesitated. His best friend's extra naps were a secret. "Well, let's just say the guy isn't the world's greatest sleeper. What if Ferret Face is making it worse?"

The question was immediately replaced by a more pressing issue. They had reached the makeshift greenhouse. The meerkat was not there.

"That's impossible!" Griffin exclaimed, refusing to believe the evidence of his own eyes. "There's no way he could lift the glass cover to get out!"

But there was also no denying that the greenhouse was empty.

Wordlessly, Savannah grabbed Griffin by the shoulders and turned him around. There, about six feet behind them, was the meerkat, up on its hind legs, watching them.

"How —?"

All at once, the animal was gone again, as suddenly as if it had vanished in a puff of smoke. Seconds later, it was back in the greenhouse, looking up at them.

Griffin was flabbergasted. "He *teleports*?"

Savannah walked over and crouched down at the spot where the meerkat had once stood. "He tunnels. I should have known. Meerkats are diggers."

Griffin was alarmed. "Then there's no way to keep him inside the greenhouse! He could dig his way out and come up anywhere! I have to lock him in a closet or something!"

Savannah smiled patiently. "Don't you see? It's just like the beaver. He's living like a meerkat in the Kalahari."

"Except in the Kalahari, he can't pop up in front of my parents!"

"Meerkats are low on the food chain," Savannah explained, "so they develop strong bonds to a safe place. If you keep plenty of food in the greenhouse, he'll always come back to it."

"That works?"

She chuckled. "Zoology isn't an exact science. Nothing is certain when you're dealing with living creatures, each with its own unique temperament. But you'll probably be okay."

He regarded her with dismay. She had complete confidence in her understanding of animal behavior. But The Man With The Plan was starting to see that no reliable plan could ever include forty animals. They were just too quirky and unpredictable.

He could feel fate closing in on him. Something was going to go wrong. The only question was when.

If there was one thing Darren Vader couldn't stand, it was to be left out of something big.

And this was big. He could smell it. Bing, his sawed-off sidekick, and their flock of sheep definitely had those animals. Somehow, they had found a way to pull off the zoobreak without him.

Griffin was a loser, but Darren had to give him credit. He obviously knew how to recognize a business opportunity. This may have started out as a rescue for Drysdale's monkey. But when Bing got aboard the zoo boat and looked around at the animals, he had to see dollar signs. What else could explain going for one critter and coming back with the whole kit and caboodle? It was all about the Benjamins — the kind of money his old man was never going to make with his fruit pickers and orchard scooters.

Darren knew he had to get in on this scam. But how? Blackmail didn't work. But he should have expected that. He had almost as much to lose here as Bing. If Darren ratted to the cops, sure, the zoobreakers would get in trouble. But then the jig would be up. The animals would go back to the paddleboat, and nobody would make a buck off them.

He walked to the window and peered out over the rooftops of Cedarville. Griffin and the others were biding their time, waiting for the right moment to cash out. That meant that somewhere hidden in this boring little town was a fortune in stolen animals. If he could somehow get his hands on one — just one . . .

A sound reached him out of the distance. A muffled — hooting? He recalled Griffin's words the previous morning: *I didn't say owl; I said towel.*

He had a grainy vision of a great horned owl asleep in its cage at *All Aboard Animals.*

Smiling now, he powered up his computer and opened the browser for a Google search. Keywords: *owl trap.*

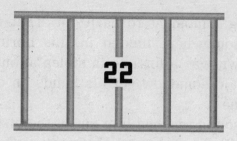

22

The cages were piled in a corner of the main compartment that had once been the floating zoo.

"It's a write-off, boss," Klaus rumbled in his deep baritone. "They've all got at least a few bars cut."

Mr. Nastase added the item to his list of losses for the insurance company: *31 state-of-the-art climate-controlled animal habitats with electronic locks.*

If he couldn't have his animals back, at least he could make a killing on the insurance claim. And there was one other advantage to the theft of his zoo. . . .

"You know," he commented, "I never thought I'd be able to breathe through my nose on this boat. I don't think I realized how bad the stink was till it was gone."

"Amen," his security man agreed. "Still, I kind of miss the little guys. I didn't think I was the type to get attached. But that's what happened with some of them."

"I don't miss a single one," the zookeeper said flatly. "I miss the lines of paying customers. I miss the feeling of their money in the cash box. I miss the sight of a spoiled brat in an *All Aboard Animals* T-shirt, overpaying for a souvenir and giving me free advertising at the same time."

Klaus laughed. "You're a hard man, boss." The smile clouded. "But there *is* one kid I'd like to see again."

"I know." The lines of Mr. Nastase's mustache sharpened to a spear point. "Ferris Atwater, Jr."

"Right, him, too, I guess. But I was thinking of the little snot-nose who went commando on me and then lured me into the ceiling."

The zookeeper added a note on the insurance paper about the damage done to the ceiling and bulkhead while cutting this muscle-bound lunkhead out of the ductwork.

Aloud, he said, "I hope you know, Klaus, how much I appreciate what you went through for this company."

His cell phone rang. From the display, he recognized the number of Detective Harrigan, the lead officer investigating the robbery.

"I hope you have some good news for me, Detective," Nastase said into the handset. "Klaus and I have been going through the wreckage here, and it hasn't exactly been fun."

"We found a few webcams we believe were used to case the boat," Harrigan replied. "Their server seems to be overseas — ultra-secure, dead end. But we've got something else that might turn into a lead. There have been reports of an aggressive owl terrorizing cats and dogs in a Long Island town not far from you. You lost an owl, didn't you?"

"Yes, a very valuable one," Nastase confirmed. "But surely there are a lot of owls on Long Island."

"The timing's a little suspicious. And the location — it's across the sound from the spot where we found your life raft. Maybe you've heard of this town — Cedarville."

Cedarville! *All Aboard Animals* booked

hundreds of school visits. But that name sounded familiar.

"Thanks, Detective. Please keep me posted." As soon as he was off the phone, the zookeeper went to the office and took out the appointment log for school tours.

There it was — Cedarville Public School District. They'd sent several groups the week before the robbery. It rang an unpleasant bell. That girl — Sabrina, Susanna, something like that. The one who'd accused him of stealing her monkey! The family had even gone so far as to have their lawyer call.

He began flipping through the register, searching for his notes on the incident.

Klaus ducked in through the hatchway. "Find something, boss?"

"That girl — the one who insisted Eleanor was hers." He slapped the page. "Here it is — Savannah Drysdale from Cedarville, New York. The same town where owl sightings are happening right now."

"Great news!" Klaus exclaimed. "Call that cop and tell him what we know."

Mr. Nastase looked thoughtful. "I don't think we should involve the police just yet. I want to handle this — quietly."

The security man was mystified. "What for?" He frowned. "Wait a minute. You're not telling me we really *did* steal that monkey?"

"Of course not!" the zookeeper replied in a wounded tone. "It's just that things can get complicated when you're dealing with false accusations."

Klaus fixed him with a piercing stare. "But we definitely didn't steal the monkey, right?"

"Do I look like a thief?"

Klaus's eyes fell on the desk lamp. The sticker on the shade read: PROPERTY OF HOLIDAY INN.

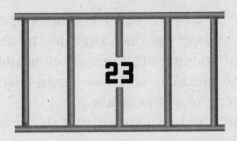

23

"Ben, are you all right?"

Ben opened his eyes to find Nurse Savage leaning over the cot where he took his special nap every day. He moved his arm across his chest to make sure she didn't notice the bump in his sweatshirt that represented Ferret Face's hiding place of the moment.

"Uh, I'm fine," he answered. "I just can't sleep."

She raised her eyebrows. "That's the whole point, isn't it? You're supposed to sleep. You've always slept before. Has anything changed in your medical condition?"

"I don't think so," Ben said carefully. Being saddled with a ferret 24/7 was definitely a condition, but it wasn't medical. The truth was painfully obvious to him. Narcolepsy or not, he was no longer in danger of falling asleep during the day. Any time he showed signs of nodding off, Ferret Face would grab hold of his skin and bite down just hard enough to keep him awake.

How could he explain *that* to the school nurse?

She had a theory. "It's almost as if you're trying to sleep, but something is preventing you from letting go. Are you having bad dreams? I distinctly heard you say 'ouch.' "

"Well, I'm definitely not sleeping, so it can't be dreams."

The nurse probed further. "How is your sleep at night?"

Ben shrugged. "I don't know. I'm asleep at the time." But the truth was, the nights were okay, since Ferret Face slept then, too. The ferret liked to crawl all the way to the end of the bed and sleep under Ben's feet. It was actually pretty comfortable — if you could ignore the fact that the room was starting to smell like *All Aboard Animals*. Mom had been giving him gentle reminders lately about using deodorant.

The nurse sighed. "Well, if this continues, I'm going to have to get in touch with your pediatrician."

Ben swallowed hard. His doctor might not be as smart as the sleep experts at the DuPont Youth Academy for Sleep Science, but he would probably notice a ferret living inside his patient's shirt.

He could feel the walls of the Health Office closing in on him. He had to talk to Griffin.

"Ah-choo!"

Logan's sneeze was completely unconvincing. He grimaced in annoyance. He was never going to get that allergy commercial if he couldn't come up with a better sneeze than that. And then Logan Kellerman would never get to be as famous as Ferris Atwater, Jr., already was.

Practice!

"Ah-choo! Ah-choo! Ah-*choo*!"

He was sneezing so loudly that he almost missed his mother's scream. By the time he ran downstairs, she was on the phone, wide-eyed and ranting:

"It's the biggest rat I've ever seen in my life! Right in my basement! There's no way those little mousetraps are going to work on this monster! Bring a shotgun!"

Heart sinking, Logan opened the door

and peered down the cellar stairs. It was too dark to make out much detail, but the beaver's eyes burned up out of the gloom, red and wild.

He had a giddy vision of the coverall-clad exterminator coming up out of the basement. "Mrs. Kellerman, you don't have rats; you've got beavers. And turtles and salamanders and frogs. In fact, you've got a lot of stuff that disappeared off that zoo boat. And your son bears a striking resemblance to Ferris Atwater, Jr.!"

This called for drastic action. As soon as his mom hung up the phone and left the room, he pounced on the handset and hit redial.

"Cedarville Pest Control," came a voice on the other end.

"Hi. Did you just get a call from the Kellerman house, 414 DeWitt? I'm calling to cancel. It was all a misunderstanding. It wasn't a rat. It was a stuffed otter. Sorry for the mix-up. Don't come."

Man, that was close! Logan didn't want to think about what might have happened if he hadn't been home.

But an hour later, he was experimenting with different combinations of pepper and smelling salts, looking for the perfect sneeze, when he heard his mother on the phone again.

"Where are you people? You said right away! . . . Cancel? Of course I didn't cancel! Why would I cancel? There's a rat downstairs that could eat my children! Come *now*!"

And when Logan called to nix the appointment yet again, the exterminator was so angry that he vowed he would refuse to come to the Kellerman house even if there was a T. rex chewing on the roof shingles.

Logan let out a breath. He was safe — for now. But there were other exterminators in other towns. Mom wasn't going to let this lie. They had to get rid of the animals. And fast!

Cleopatra was the first to sense that something was not right. She danced nervously around the kitchen, swinging on the cabinet knobs, chattering in agitation.

"What is it, Cleo?" Savannah asked. "What's wrong?"

Ding-dong.

The monkey jumped into Savannah's arms and clung there, trembling.

"Come on, sweetie, we'll see who it is."

She threw the front door wide open. There stood Mr. Nastase and Klaus.

"I knew it!" the zookeeper exclaimed in triumph. "I knew I'd find Eleanor here!"

Savannah slammed the door in their faces. *"Dad!"*

In a split second, Mr. Drysdale was at her side. He opened the door again. "Is there any reason why you two are trespassing on our property?"

"That monkey was stolen from my zoo!" Mr. Nastase said coldly.

"I'll tell you what you told our lawyer a couple of weeks ago," said Mr. Drysdale. "All capuchins look alike, and you can't prove this one is yours. My daughter's pet was lost, and now she's home. That's all that matters here."

"Your daughter is a criminal," the zookeeper accused. "She was part of a group of juvenile delinquents who broke into my zoo and stole forty valuable animals!"

Mr. Drysdale was blown away. "Who do you think she is — Jesse James? Savannah and her friends are eleven years old! They're no more capable of pulling off what happened at your zoo than they are of flying to the moon!"

"The kid who attacked me was half the size of her," rumbled Klaus.

"Look," said Mr. Drysdale, "we're animal lovers. We have a lot of pets. But don't you think I'd notice if there were forty extras around?"

"That depends" — Mr. Nastase's mustache was nearly two parallel lines — "on how hard you look at what's *right under your nose!*" He reached for the capuchin in Savannah's arms.

Cleopatra let out a shriek of terror.

With a *woof* that shook the very foundations of the house, a large, dark shape leaped over the fence from the backyard. By the time Luthor's big paws hit the grass, he was in full flight, bounding up the front walk to come to the aid of his dearest friend.

Klaus caught sight of the Doberman first. He picked up Mr. Nastase and hoisted him away from the front door. A heartbeat later, Luthor landed on that very spot.

"Run, boss!"

The two took off out of the yard and down the street. If Savannah hadn't called off her dog, Luthor would have pursued them to the ends of the earth.

The zookeeper and his security man were

still running when they reached their rental car. They threw themselves inside and locked the doors.

"Thank you for that quick thinking, Klaus!" Mr. Nastase panted. "I can't believe they sicced that monster on us!"

"I think the monkey did that!" Klaus gasped. "It was her voice that brought the dog."

Still shaken, the zookeeper opened his window. The angry barking had stopped. "The coast is clear."

Klaus looked puzzled. "I thought Eleanor would be happy to be rescued. But she seemed pretty comfortable with the kid."

Mr. Nastase was disgusted. "A dumb animal is comfortable with anybody who feeds it."

"*We* used to feed her," Klaus pointed out, "but she sure didn't like it when you got too close. Those people have it wrong, huh? You definitely didn't steal her?"

"Of course not. I bought her from a reputable animal dealer."

"Yeah, but how did the dealer get her?" Klaus probed.

The zookeeper was annoyed. "Your job, Klaus, is security — which you might have done better, since all our exhibits are gone.

You let me worry about the animals. I know everything there is to know about each and every one of them."

From the waterfowl pond in the park next to the Drysdale home, the loon yodeled its distinctive mournful call.

"Filthy pigeons," Mr. Nastase commented. "Rats with wings."

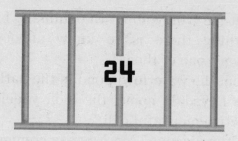

24

When Griffin arrived at school the next morning, the sight that met his eyes nearly stopped his heart. There, seated in the glassed-in outer office, was Mr. Nastase.

Oh, no!

Since the zoobreak, the one thing that had been going in their favor was the fact that the search for the missing animals was taking place in Connecticut. But now Mr. Nasty had found Cedarville. And Dr. Alford and her baboons were not due back for another eight days.

Don't panic, Griffin told himself. *It's just him; no cops. He doesn't know anything for sure.*

When he found the note in his locker, he was certain it was his summons to the office for a face-to-face grilling by the zookeeper. But it wasn't from the principal. He unfolded the paper and read:

EMERGENCY MEETING!
THE BALLROOM! NOW!

The ballroom was Coach Nimitz's graveyard for all the broken balls and equipment he couldn't bring himself to throw in the garbage. Griffin headed down the hallway behind the gym and slipped into the storage room. They were all there, up to their knees in flattened sports gear — Savannah, Pitch, Logan, Melissa, and Ben.

Griffin addressed his best friend first. "I was wondering why I didn't see you on the way to school."

Ben looked contrite. "Sorry to gang up on you, Griffin, but everybody agrees. We've got to get rid of the animals before it's too late."

Griffin nodded in resignation. "I was going to call a meeting anyway. Mr. Nasty is in the principal's office."

"Forget that!" Savannah was close to the edge. "He was at my *house* yesterday! Griffin, he *knows*!"

"He *suspects*," Griffin amended. "But remember — that's Nastase in the office, not the police. He doesn't want the cops nosing around because he doesn't want it to come out that he stole Cleopatra in the first place."

"Are you saying that we're safe?" Pitch asked incredulously.

"No," Griffin admitted. "When he finds out exactly where the animals are, and who's got them, *that's* when he'll go to the cops — when it's an open-and-shut case and we're the crooks, not him. That means there's still time."

"No!" The word was spoken with such force that no one believed it had come from quiet, shy Melissa. "Please! No more time! My baby brother is afraid of stuffed animals because one of them moved! My mother found an egg in my slippers! It can't go on!"

"Amen to that!" said Logan. "I can't call every exterminator on Long Island and tell them my mother's crazy!"

"We got our electric bill," Ben put in. "It was over seven hundred dollars! My family's going broke just to keep the sauna running for the chuckwalla!"

"Our garage is starting to smell like a barn," Pitch complained.

"I hear you," Griffin said sadly. "I'm having problems, too, you know. The meerkat tunneled into Mrs. Abernathy's vegetable garden. Lucky for us the cops thought she was reporting a 'mere cat' rather than a 'meerkat.' That was a close one."

"Well, what are you going to do about it?" Pitch demanded. "Sooner or later we're going to run out of these lucky breaks."

"We need a plan," Griffin concluded. "Something that gets the animals out of our hair and into a safe place until Dr. Alford comes back from baboon shopping."

Savannah was depressed. "It sounds great, but it's not so simple. These are living creatures. They need to be cared for, fed, and exercised. The predators have to be separated from the prey. They make noises and smells. We'll never find a place like that."

"Not without starting our own zoo," Pitch agreed glumly.

And suddenly, The Man With The Plan was living up to his name.

"That's it!" he exclaimed. "A second zoobreak! We broke them out of one zoo — we'll break them into another! We'll take them to the Long Island Zoo, and they'll be waiting there when Dr. Alford gets back!"

Ben was appalled. "Are you crazy? That's no little paddleboat with cages they bought at Wal-Mart! That's a *real* zoo with *real* security!"

Savannah looked thoughtful and hopeful at the same time. "You know — I'm not saying it's going to be easy, but Dr. Alford once took me there when it was shut down for the night. The buildings are locked electronically." She looked meaningfully at Melissa. "It's all run by computer from the main office."

"I'll do anything!" Melissa promised. "Just so I can have my bedroom back!"

"And my basement," Logan put in.

"And my garage," added Pitch.

Ben was bitter. "You don't think I want my sauna back? And to wear a shirt that doesn't have a ferret in it? But this is crazy! You push the wrong button, and you could send a herd of elephants stampeding down the Long Island Expressway!"

"We'll be careful," Savannah promised. "Don't you see? This is the best idea in the world! We're saved!"

"Not yet," Pitch said grimly. "How are we going to get there? That zoo must be ten miles away. We can't bike there carrying all the animals. And it's not near the water, so a boat doesn't help us."

A slow smile replaced Griffin's worried expression — the smile that said the new plan was beginning to take shape.

Mr. Nastase and Klaus were sharing a Formica table at Mr. Pizza Guy when the waitress set a basket down between them.

"What's this?" the zookeeper asked, frowning.

"Cheezie Stix."

"We didn't order anything else," Klaus told her.

She grinned. "Compliments of the young gentleman at the counter."

Darren Vader swiveled on his stool and fired off a snappy salute.

"Man," said Klaus under his breath, "is this kid for real?"

Darren left the counter and joined them at their table, helping himself to a Cheezie Stik as he sat down. "Darren Vader," he introduced himself. "I have a business proposition. I set out an owl trap a couple of days ago. Interested to see if I caught anything?"

Klaus's hand shot up from beneath the table, grabbed Darren's elbow, and squeezed. "You're some piece of work, trying to sell us back our own animals!"

"Hey, that hurts!"

Mr. Nastase leaned into the boy's face. "Now I have a proposition for you. Why don't we go down to the police station, and you tell them what other traps you've set?"

Darren gulped. "It's just the owl! Honest!"

Mr. Nastase's civilized veneer faded as his temper rose. "I wasn't born yesterday, kid! I know you're mixed up with Savannah Drysdale and Ferris Atwater, Jr., and the gang of delinquents who emptied my zoo!"

"I'm not!" Darren quavered.

Klaus squeezed harder.

"Okay, I was part of the team at first, but I didn't go! I couldn't get out that night! I really did use an owl trap! I bought it on eBay! I'll show you the receipt!"

"I've got a better idea, *Darren Vader*," said the zookeeper. "You can show me the owl. And then you can tell me where to find the rest of my animals."

"Aren't you going to pay me anything?" Darren pleaded.

"Certainly," Mr. Nastase agreed. "If you help me get my zoo back, I will reward you by not telling the police that you're the one who robbed my place of business."

Darren was horrified. "But I'm innocent!"

"Possibly. But who will believe it when they see you have my owl?"

"That's not fair!" Darren wailed.

"Life isn't fair," the zookeeper commiserated. "But it can be bearable — if you cooperate."

Poor Darren could not understand how things had gone so terribly wrong. He had come here with a valuable owl to sell, and Mr. Nastase had managed to turn everything against him. All he could do was nod miserably. He didn't dare speak for fear he would dig himself an even deeper hole.

Mr. Nastase nibbled triumphantly on a Cheezie Stik. "You've got twenty-four hours to find out where your former associates are hiding my animals." He smacked his lips. "These are really good."

25

OPERATION ZOOBREAK II

DATE: Wednesday, April 15
TIME: midnight sharp
INSTRUCTIONS: bring cargo, SECURELY
PACKED, to the meeting point for transport to Long
Island Zoo

There was a knock at the door. "Ben?" came Mr. Slovak's voice. "Can I come in?"

"Just a minute, Dad." Ben stuffed Ferret Face into his closet along with his printout of tomorrow night's plan. He opened the door to admit his father. "What's up?"

"I have some news." Mr. Slovak's expression was solemn. "DuPont Academy just called. There's a place opening up for you in ten days."

Ben had known this was coming, but he hadn't expected to be so devastated by the reality. He told himself he ought to be happy. He was going to be safe in New Jersey, where there were no zoobreaks, either into or out of captivity. He should have been relieved that at least the suspense was over — no more sword dangling above his head. Instead, all he thought about was a boarding school he didn't want to go to, far away from everything he knew and cared about, far away from his best friend. Being shanghaied into his second zoobreak in a week now seemed like a minor inconvenience compared with that.

He took a deep breath. "Okay. So what do I have to do?"

"Nothing right away," Mr. Slovak replied sympathetically. "I just wanted to let you know it was coming. And by the way, the school nurse called. She says your nap habits have changed, and she wants you to see Dr. Patterson."

Ben sighed. "Sure, why not?" After tomorrow night, Ferret Face would be history, and he would be back to normal . . . or, at least, normal for a kid with narcolepsy.

When his father left, Ben opened the closet door. "All right, Ferret Face. The coast is clear." He stared. The ferret was chewing on the plan for Zoobreak II! He made a grab for the paper, but the agile creature darted underneath his hand and out into the bedroom.

"Give me that!" he hissed. He took a flying leap onto his bed, but the ferret scooted just out of his grasp. It scrambled across the pillow and jumped back down to the carpet. As it passed the open window, a strong breeze tore the page from its mouth and tossed it into the yard.

"Now look what you've done!" A live plan blowing around the neighborhood — Griffin would have a heart attack.

Ben took the stairs three at a time and burst through the back door. The paper was nowhere to be seen.

Oh, well, if I can't find it, no one else can. It's probably stuck twenty feet up a tree.

Griffin didn't have to know about this . . . or about DuPont Academy. The Man With The Plan had enough on his mind.

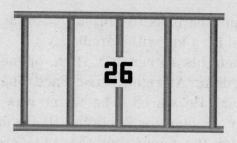

26

Wednesday, April 15, dawned brilliant and sunny. Nowhere was brighter than the Cedarville Marina, where Mr. Vader's boat, the *In-Vader*, was docked in slip 19.

Darren emerged from the cabin below, hauling a square wire-mesh cage. In it, blinking his huge yellow eyes in confusion and discomfort, was Hoo.

Klaus took the trap from him and peered at its occupant. "That's him, all right. Good to see you, little buddy."

Mr. Nastase barely glanced in the owl's direction. "That's only half of our bargain. Now, where are the rest of my animals?"

Darren shook his head. "I don't know."

The zookeeper's eyes narrowed. "Do you have any idea what life is like inside a juvenile detention center?"

Darren gulped. "I don't know where they are now, but I know where they'll be tonight." From his pocket he produced a much-rumpled paper and began to unfold it carefully. The heading read:

OPERATION ZOOBREAK II

Klaus frowned. "Zoobreak? What is this — a joke?"

"This kid Griffin is a really big idiot," Darren explained. "He writes up a plan like this every time he goes to the bathroom."

"And you got the paper from him?" Mr. Nastase probed.

Darren shook his head. "From his sawed-off sidekick. I was spying on his house, trying to see if he had any of the animals. This blew out the window."

The security man ran his finger along the bumpy contours of the sheet's missing corner. "Bite marks," he concluded. "Small ones."

His boss scanned the page in anger.

"They're taking *my* animals to someone else's zoo! We'll just see about that!"

The meerkat stood on the dresser once more, watching intently as Griffin plucked the gerbils, hamsters, and mice out from among the Lego pieces and zipped them into a small backpack.

He selected a toothpick from the box and peered into the plastic drawers to begin the distasteful task of cleanup. Then, with a sigh, he took the entire collection and dumped it into a large green garbage bag. He was getting too old for Lego anyway.

Hey, if the worst thing that happened out of all this was the loss of a little Lego, they would be getting off easy. Who would have thought that a few helpless animals would be harder to handle than a million-dollar baseball card? But you could plan for a card. With animals, the plan was always changing. From one rescue to forty. From a breakout to a secret hotel operation. And now Zoobreak II, the riskiest plan of all.

"Can we pull it off?" he asked aloud.

The meerkat didn't know, either. But he was a good listener, this mongoose cousin.

He sat up on his hind legs and always seemed to be paying such rapt attention. And, Griffin reflected, there was no chance of him spilling the beans. That was pure gold.

"Cracker?" It was a rhetorical question. The meerkat never turned down a Ritz.

Griffin and his companion shared a tense pre-zoobreak snack. He hoped they served these at the Long Island Zoo. He should make an anonymous call about it to Dr. Alford when she got back from Africa.

Thinking ahead to a time after tonight was almost impossible. The next few hours would be the most difficult of their lives.

The grandfather clock in the dining room chimed midnight. Griffin peered out the window. A shadowy figure lurked near the rosebush: Pitch, with a backpack of her own and a wicker picnic basket. Operation Zoobreak II was on.

He hustled the meerkat into a canvas draw-string bag, shouldered his cargo, and crept silently down the stairs and out the front door. By that time, Melissa was there, too, with her wagon on which sat three wriggling laundry bags. Ben traveled light with the chuckwalla in a zipper pocket and Ferret Face inside his shirt. But Logan required a duffel for his beaver, turtles, salamanders, and frogs. Last of all, carrying the heaviest burden, came Savannah with rabbits, white rats, duck, and loon in four pet carriers.

Griffin stared at her matted hair and dripping clothes. "Why are you all wet?"

"The loon wouldn't leave!" Savannah spluttered. "I had to go into the water and get him!"

"Okay, Griffin," said Pitch. "We're all here, and so is the livestock. How do we get to the zoo?"

In answer, Griffin eased open the garage door. There stood the six prototypes of his father's newest invention, all charged up and ready to go.

Logan was blown away. "What are they?"

Griffin jumped onto the riding platform of the first one. "Presenting the SmartPick Rollo-Bushel." He wheeled out of the garage, executing quick turns in and around the team. "Titanium frame construction, pinpoint steering, animal-friendly bushel basket, and good for fifty miles on a single charge."

Pitch was delighted. "This is awesome!" She hopped onto her unit and put it through its paces, spinning around experimentally.

"Your dad's pretty weird, but man, he invents some wild stuff!"

"Tell that to Mrs. Vader," said Griffin. "She doesn't think the Rollo-Bushel is unique enough to deserve its own patent."

Ben made a face. "Big talk, considering the only thing she's ever given the world is Darren." He touched the handlebar and immediately drove into the garage wall. "Ow!"

"Careful!" Griffin hissed. "If anything happens to one of these prototypes, my dad will ground me till I'm ninety. All right, load up the animals. And don't forget to take a bike helmet."

Anyone who happened to be looking out the window that night would have been treated to an amazing sight: a line of eleven-year-olds, standing ramrod-straight on moving platforms, rolling silently down the street.

Traffic was light, but every single passing car slowed down to stare. A teenager in a pickup truck lowered his window and called, "How much do you want for one of those?"

"They're not for sale," Griffin replied from his position in the lead.

"Do you think we look *cool*?" Melissa mused in amazement. "I've never been cool before."

"Are you kidding?" Pitch laughed. "We belong on the cover of *Dorks Illustrated*!"

"But if you need to move a meerkat," Griffin tossed back, "this is better than a Lamborghini." In spite of the crushing gravity of the task ahead, he couldn't help but feel pride in his father's invention.

At the Rollo-Bushel's top speed of twelve miles per hour, they floated south along the shoulder of County Road 47, past closed strip malls and darkened neighborhoods.

Griffin was terrified that a police officer would cruise by and wonder what six kids were doing out at this hour on such bizarre vehicles. But luck stayed with them, and the cops patrolled other roads. Even the animals were cooperative. Most of them took the darkness of night as a signal that they should be sleeping.

They'd been traveling for nearly an hour before the headlamp on Griffin's prototype illuminated a sign:

LONG ISLAND ZOOLOGICAL GARDEN
NEXT RIGHT

"This is it, you guys! Follow me!"

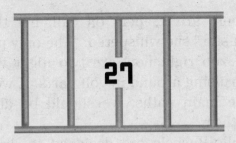

27

A zoo was such a daytime place that it seemed eerie and threatening in the gloom. The team wheeled through acres of empty parking lot, illuminated only by the faintest of lights. The ticket windows were shuttered, the front gate barred by a rolling section of fence.

Pitch hopped off her Rollo-Bushel and scaled the barrier with ease. "Piece of cake," she called softly. "It's just a latch."

Griffin helped her slide the heavy fencing aside, and the six vehicles entered the zoo.

From here, Savannah took over the lead role in the operation. Not only was she the animal expert, but she had been here after hours. Dr. Alford had given her an insider's view.

"There are keepers on call, but they're not on site," she whispered. "The only people at the zoo right now are two night watchmen cruising around in golf carts. If we stay off the main paths, we should be able to avoid them."

"Rollo-Bushels are designed to drive in orchards," Griffin added. "We can take them on the grass."

Melissa spoke up. "Where's the computer that controls the cage locks?"

"In the administration building," Savannah replied. "It's just past the food court."

The procession of Rollo-Bushels drove off the pavement into the cover of the trees. They skirted the compound, their vehicles bumping over stones and roots. The ride was rougher, but the suspension was rock steady. The bags with their live cargo shook but did not fall off.

Their course took them behind some of the zoo's more famous exhibits. Griffin could make out the tall shape of a sleeping giraffe silhouetted against a moonlit sky. Farther along were two huge hulks, probably the rounded backs of elephants. But this was no sightseeing tour. He couldn't let his mind wander now that their goal was so close at hand. He focused all his attention on keeping his scooter right behind Savannah's and making sure the others were close behind him.

ADMINISTRATION read the sign in front of a low building constructed in the shape of an L. It lay flat to the ground, its front door protected by a simple padlock.

Griffin stopped his Rollo-Bushel, hopped off the platform, and approached the entrance. From the side pouch of his backpack, he produced the wire cutters he'd used to open the cages in the first zoobreak. He clamped the blades around the lock and squeezed. No progress. Pitch came to lend her strength to the task. The two of them groaned with effort. Still nothing.

Savannah was alarmed. "If we can't get into the office, we'll never be able to turn off the electronic locks!"

"You mean we came all this way for *nothing*?" asked Logan, aghast. "No way am I taking that beaver back to my basement!"

Griffin abandoned the wire cutters. "Any good plan includes backup." He reached into the pouch once more and pulled out a small hacksaw. "This'll take a few minutes. Stash the Rollo-Bushels in the bushes just in case the security guards come by."

He went to work on the padlock, sawing vigorously. It was slow going, and soon he was bathed in sweat despite the cool night. The metal gave way, bit by bit, the shavings raining down on the stoop. Finally, the lock clattered to the pavement. They were in.

Griffin, Savannah, and Melissa entered, leaving the others to guard the animals. The inside of the building could have been the main office at school, with desks and cubicles and small meeting rooms down a hallway.

"Okay," said Griffin, all business. "Which computer unlocks the cages?"

"They all will," said Melissa. "The system has to be run on a secure intranet. Any networked station should do the job."

"We'll use the one in Dr. Alford's office," Savannah decided. "She definitely has the authority." She led them down the corridor to the door marked CURATOR.

The door was ajar, the computer still on and humming. Melissa sat down and began to pound the keyboard.

"Do you think she can do it?" wondered Savannah, her eyes full of anxiety.

"I don't know," Griffin replied. "But on a computer, if Melissa can't do it, it can't be done."

They stood in silence as the keyboard clattered and data flashed across the screen. The tension was so dense that it was almost visible in the room. The weight of this whole affair was especially heavy on Savannah, since the theft of her monkey had set it all in motion. And as for Griffin, he knew that no hacksaw could save the plan if they couldn't access the cages. Worse, there was no going back — not to Savannah's shed, Logan's basement, Melissa's closet, Pitch's garage, Ben's sauna, or Griffin's Lego.

Melissa's quiet voice startled both of them. "Okay," she said, "which cage do you want to open first?"

The judge's gavel came down like a pistol shot. "I sentence you to fifty years in juvenile detention!"

"*No-o-o-o!*" cried Darren, devastated. "I'm innocent!" He wheeled in the courtroom to face Mr. Nastase, who was laughing loudly in the front row, Klaus at his side. "You know I'm innocent!"

"You should have thought of that before sending us on a wild goose chase to the Long Island Zoo!" Mr. Nastase jeered.

"It's Bing's fault!" Darren babbled. "He and Slovak set me up! They dropped that fake plan out the window because they saw me spying on the house!"

"Bailiff!" thundered the judge. "Take him away."

Darren tried to escape, but strong hands grabbed him, shaking him.

"Let me go!"

"Darren — Darren, wake up! You're having a nightmare."

Shocked, Darren opened his eyes. The arms that held him tightly were his mother's. His father was by the light switch, looking worried.

His relief that the fifty-year sentence had been only a dream evaporated when his mother asked, "You were spying on *what* house?"

Uh-oh. "I don't know. It was just a dream. I don't even remember what it was about."

"You were babbling about Griffin and Ben," his mother informed him. "And you kept saying you were innocent. I know you, Darren

186

Vader. You're *never* innocent. What are you mixed up in this time?"

Darren was too sleepy and too rattled to think up a good lie. He blurted out the whole ugly truth.

His father was horrified. "Are you telling me that six kids are all the way out at that zoo at one-thirty in the morning, and you sent two thugs after them?"

It sounded bad, even to Darren. "I had no choice! They were going to call the cops on me because I had a hot owl!"

Mrs. Vader cast her husband a stricken look. "We have to call those other parents — *and* the police."

28

Griffin and Ben parked their Rollo-Bushels in the shadows behind the Small Mammal House. Ben unloaded the pet carrier containing the rabbits and the laundry bag with the prairie dog. Griffin hefted the drawstring sack where his meerkat lay sleeping.

"Team One to Base," he said into his walkie-talkie. "Melissa, we're at Small Mammals. Pop the door."

"Got it," came Melissa's voice. "Let's hope this works."

They stood, barely daring to breathe, and almost broke into wild celebration when they heard a loud click. Griffin reached for the handle and pulled the door wide.

"We're in."

Logan's voice came over the speaker from Base. "Tell me when the beaver's gone."

"The beaver's with Team Two at North American Wetlands," Griffin said briskly. "Savannah and Pitch are dumping him with the duck and the loon."

They found themselves in a long corridor with glassed-in habitats on both sides. Most of the animals were asleep, their displays dark. The main hall was in night mode, bathed in reddish light.

Ben radiated anxiety. "How do we get them into the habitats? If we break the glass, we'll have the whole zoo on our necks!"

On the other side of the grounds, at North American Wetlands, Savannah overheard them on her own walkie-talkie.

"There's a hallway in back that lets you get into the displays," she advised. "Look for an entrance marked 'Staff Only.'"

"Got it," Griffin confirmed. "It's locked. Melissa?"

"Hang on." A moment later, there was a telltale click.

Ben pushed the door open, and they hustled their bags inside. This hallway was a thin passage that extended the full length of the building behind the row of habitats. They could not see into the displays, but each one had an access panel that was clearly marked. It identified the animals inside, their food and water requirements, and maintenance instructions.

Griffin went along, reading the signs. "Here — Eastern Cottontail Rabbit." He opened the panel just a crack, and they peered inside. There in the middle of the tall grass and pebbly sand of the habitat slumbered two gray-brown bundles of fur.

Ben was dismayed. "Our guys are white! We've got the wrong rabbits!"

"They'll do," Griffin decided. "Savannah said it doesn't have to be a perfect match. They just have to avoid killing each other before the zoo people notice them in the morning."

They took the three rabbits out of the carrier and placed them gently into the habitat. The new arrivals, their sleep disturbed, looked around with bleary eyes but soon settled down. If they were agitated by the move, it didn't show.

Griffin felt a faint stirring of hope. The first animals had been unloaded. This could work. It *would* work. . . .

A few displays down, they deposited the prairie dog into a dusty enclosure with tumbleweeds and two others of its species.

Switching to the other side of the hall, they located the meerkat exhibit. The heat was cranked up so high that it baked the moisture right out of their eyes as they placed the former tenant of Mrs. Bing's greenhouse into its natural habitat.

"You know," said Griffin in a subdued voice, "I'm going to miss that little guy. I know it sounds crazy, but sometimes I felt he was the only one who really understood me."

"You're right," Ben told him. "It sounds crazy."

That left Ferret Face. In the very last enclosure, they found a community that included a black-footed ferret, two stoats, a European polecat, and a weasel.

Ben reached into his hoodie and pulled Ferret Face out. "Okay, buddy, this is your stop."

It was one thing to find a home for Ferret Face; it was quite another to make him go into it. It took every ounce of strength the two had to disconnect the ferret's claws from the fleece of the hoodie. Even then, the creature tried to wrestle his way out of Ben's hands, wriggling and spitting. He was just a few inches from the opening when he suddenly froze, eyes fixed inside the display. There, looking out at him, displaying similar markings, was another ferret — a little larger, but otherwise identical.

Seizing the moment, Ben placed Ferret Face onto the grass, and the two new friends scurried off together. Ben stared after them for a long moment.

"They grow up so fast," he commented, only half joking.

Griffin was speaking to Melissa over the walkie-talkie once more. "Team One — all done here. Next stop, Rodent World."

They let themselves out of the building and were almost instantly pinpointed in approaching headlights. Desperately, Griffin grabbed Ben around the shoulders and hurled the two of them off the doorstep and into the bushes. They huddled there, watching in trepidation as a golf cart rattled slowly up, a uniformed security guard at the wheel. When he stopped his cart, the front tire was barely a yard from their hiding place.

Griffin switched off his walkie-talkie. If

one of the others tried to make contact now, the jig would be up.

A shiny black boot stepped right in front of his nose.

Oh, please, don't look down!

The guard walked over to the Small Mammal House and tried the door. In that heart-stopping instant, Griffin realized he had no idea if the electronic lock had reset itself. If the building was open, the guard would know something was wrong.

Locked! He and Ben exchanged a very quiet high five.

The guard got back in his golf cart and drove off.

Savannah and Pitch lurked in the shadows, waiting for the familiar click that would tell them Melissa had released the aviary door. They entered the structure, a huge open area, landscaped and treed, enclosed by mesh fencing. It was a boisterous place by day, but now the birds were merely dozens of dark shapes perched on the branches, asleep.

"This makes no sense at all," complained Pitch. "Why would you leave a chicken that can't even fly in an aviary?"

"Because they don't have a henhouse," Savannah replied. "At least here there's bird-seed and no predators."

"Unless you're a worm," Pitch agreed. She opened a laundry bag, and the hen emerged in a ponderous chicken-gait. The bird let out a slow, squawking cluck, as if testing to see if her vocal cords still worked in these strange surroundings.

The sound provoked an instant response from another bag. The fabric began to undulate in Savannah's arms. A split second later, the piglet exploded out of the drawstring opening. He hit the ground scrambling and rushed over to cuddle up to the hen.

"I guess Melissa's closet was their first date," Pitch commented.

"I was going to let him loose in the butter-fly exhibit," said Savannah, "but he'd have no one to talk to."

"You should seek help," Pitch advised, matter-of-factly.

"He'll be fine here till morning," Savannah concluded. She took out her walkie-talkie. "Team Two. We're all done. How are you making out, Griffin?"

"We're finishing in Rodent World," Griffin

replied. "We're a little behind schedule. We got hung up by a security guard."

"We saw one, too," Savannah confirmed. "He was heading out toward the Monkey House."

"We'll be done after the Reptile Center," Griffin promised. "Meet you back at Base."

In Dr. Alford's office in Administration, Melissa set down her walkie-talkie and scrolled through screens until she found the controls for the Reptile/Amphibian Center. This would be the last drop-off. Operation Zoobreak II was almost complete.

Logan put a hand on her shoulder. "If one guard is out by the monkeys, and the other is circling in a golf cart, who are those two guys?"

Melissa followed his pointing finger. A pair of dark silhouettes moved across the central path, flashlights bobbing.

Logan snatched up the walkie-talkie. "Watch it, you guys. There may be two extra security guards out there."

They didn't look like security guards to Melissa. They looked like trouble.

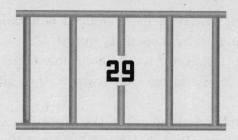

29

The design of the Reptile/Amphibian Center was similar to that of the Small Mammal House. The same night-mode bulbs cast a reddish glow over the main corridor of glassed-in displays and the narrow access halls behind them.

But the task was nowhere near as simple. After a brief scan of the habitats, Griffin went straight to the walkie-talkie.

"Team One to Savannah — where are you?"

"On our way back to Base," came the reply. "What's up?"

"The exhibits don't match what we've got," Griffin explained, worried. "There are no garter snakes, and there must be six different frog cases. Plus, the zoo turtles' heads are bigger than our whole turtles!"

"And no chuckwalla," Ben added urgently. "I think Mr. Nasty made him up."

Savannah was all business. "You're going to have to improvise — find combinations that aren't perfect but are at least safe until the zookeepers get here tomorrow. Tell me about some of the displays near you."

"This big one's got plenty of room for everybody," Ben called. "Let me check — American Alligator."

"No!" Savannah barked. "They'll snap up everything that moves, including you guys if you're not fast enough!"

They did a survey of the corridor, providing her with a list of their options. The garter snakes went in with the Chiapas Highland ribbon snake. They were cousins, Savannah explained. A forest marshlands habitat became home to the turtles, frogs, and salamanders. There were several small species there that could coexist without harming one another. And the chuckwalla they placed in a desert diorama with a Gila monster.

"You'll like it here," Ben assured his former houseguest. "It's just like our sauna, only my dad doesn't have to pay the heating bill."

Griffin shut the access panel and set the

latch in place. The flood of emotion that washed over him was like nothing he had ever experienced before. In his long and storied career as The Man With The Plan, he had known triumph, dismay, betrayal, anger, and joy. But the feeling that overwhelmed him at that moment was pure relief. The last week had piled disaster on top of disaster, but finally there was light at the end of the tunnel.

"I can't believe we did it," he marveled. "The way things have been going, I figured we'd be trampled by wildebeests, eaten by lions, or at least arrested. I guess we finally caught a break."

"Yeah," Ben mumbled in a hollow tone. "Lucky us."

Griffin frowned at his best friend. "You look like you're at a funeral. We're animal free! All we have to do is get the Rollo-Bushels home, and we're in the clear! What are you moping about?"

"The plan," Ben said unhappily. "It's over."

"Then you should be twice as happy, considering you complained louder than anybody, except maybe Logan."

"Yeah," Ben mourned. "But this wasn't

just a plan. It was the *last* plan — for me, anyway."

"What are you talking about? There's always another —" Griffin stopped short. "The academy?"

Ben nodded in misery. "I didn't want to distract you in the middle of Zoobreak Two. A spot opened up for me. I leave in nine days."

Griffin was struck dumb, the taste of victory turning to ashes in his mouth. His skill as a planner had become so advanced that he felt he could accomplish anything. But now he had to face the fact that he was powerless to save his best friend. It was no longer a matter of possibly or someday. It was a done deal, a tragedy waiting at the end of a nine-day ticking clock. He couldn't even bring himself to say, "It won't be so bad," because it was so bad already.

Their sad silence was interrupted when the door from the main hallway burst open. The two red-haloed figures that were suddenly upon them were tall and menacing in their dark clothing.

"You!" shouted Griffin and Mr. Nastase at the same time.

The shadow behind the zookeeper was enormous, and for a wild instant, Griffin thought it might be an escapee from the bear exhibit next door. But Ben knew better. It was far scarier than a bear.

Klaus.

Griffin was astounded. He'd always known that a hundred things could go wrong with the second zoobreak — their parents, zoo security, the police, the unpredictable animals. Yet never had he imagined that Mr. Nasty might be dogging their steps.

The zookeeper regarded Griffin and Ben with something approaching admiration. "You're quite a resourceful pair, aren't you? Not a zoo you can't get into, not an animal you can't steal. Well, you've come to the end of the road, my young friends. *All Aboard Animals* will be back up and running within a week."

"You're too late," Griffin shot back. "Your whole collection is stashed around the zoo. It'll take days to go through every cage and habitat."

Mr. Nastase laughed dryly. "I don't need *those* animals. I just need animals. In fact, this might be an excellent chance to upgrade my stock."

Ben was horrified. "What do you mean, upgrade?"

"It's all the same to me, so long as the cash box stays full," the zookeeper said cheerfully. "More variety means happier customers. They have an excellent selection here."

"Boss!" Klaus exclaimed in shock. "You're not thinking of stealing animals from this place!"

"Your problem, Klaus, is that you don't recognize a business opportunity when you see one." From a pocket of his long black coat, Mr. Nastase removed a compact tranquilizer gun with the first dart loaded and ready.

Unobserved, Griffin reached into his pocket and pressed the transmit button on his walkie-talkie.

Savannah and Pitch raced into the main building and arrived breathless at Dr. Alford's office.

"We're done," Savannah reported. "Where are Griffin and Ben?"

"Shhhh!"

Melissa and Logan sat paralyzed around their walkie-talkie, listening to the drama unfolding in the Reptile/Amphibian Center. The new arrivals crouched beside them.

"What is it?" Pitch whispered.

Melissa's eyes were wide with terror. "Mr. Nasty and Klaus! They've caught Griffin and Ben. And now they're going to steal animals to restock their zoo!"

"No!" Savannah cried.

Klaus's deep voice rattled the tinny speaker. "So that's the way it is, huh, boss? You lied to me. You've been boosting animals all along. That girl was telling the truth about Eleanor?"

"If you're asking if I broke into the Drysdale girl's yard and took the monkey, the answer is no," the zookeeper replied. "But I like a bargain, so I didn't ask the people who sold it to me where they got it."

"Buying a stolen monkey is just as bad as stealing it yourself!" Griffin piped up, outraged.

"The kid's right, boss," Klaus rumbled.

Mr. Nastase's reply was full of scorn. "I'd expect it from the brat — but you, Klaus? Since when are you such a Boy Scout? Make sure these two don't get away. I'm going shopping."

Savannah was full of fury. "We can't let them kidnap any more animals!"

"Hold on," Pitch said seriously. "Saving animals is fine, but our first job is to save Griffin and Ben."

"We have to do both," Savannah insisted. "To Mr. Nasty, this is like being a kid in a candy shop. He could take half the zoo. Who knows how many animals could end up on that awful boat of his?"

Logan was panicky. "But how can we stop them? That's Klaus over there. He could kill us all with his little finger."

Fearful glances passed among the four. It made no sense to fight over who they should rescue when the real issue was whether they could rescue anybody, including themselves. How could mere kids overpower Mr. Nastase and his giant of a security man?

The answer came from, of all people, shy Melissa. "What would Griffin do?" she said, her beady eyes open and alert. "We need a plan."

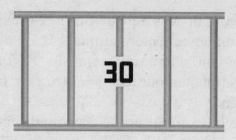

30

In the reddish glow, Griffin and Ben watched in horror as Mr. Nastase unlatched an access door that led to the corner habitat, the largest and most elaborate in the Reptile/ Amphibian Center.

Even Klaus was uneasy. "American alligator? Boss — they'll *eat* you!"

"Don't be so dramatic." The zookeeper hefted his tranquilizer pistol and ducked through the low doorway.

Griffin took a stab at reasoning with the burly security man. "You can't let him do this! This is a public zoo!"

"Quiet, kid!" Klaus looked torn, his eyes darting back and forth from his young captives to his boss, tiptoeing inside the alligator habitat. "Don't think I've forgotten what happened on the paddleboat." His threatening gaze fell on Ben. "And *you* I remember all too well."

Ben let out a whimper.

The two friends peered anxiously into the enclosure, not sure what to hope for. At any moment, one of the large reptiles could spring, snapping lethal jaws at the zookeeper. But the gators seemed content to watch, still as statues, as Mr. Nastase steered around them. All at once, he bent low, and when he straightened up again, he was holding a baby alligator, about three feet long. His fist was clamped tight on the animal's snout, immobilizing the jaws.

"He's crazy," murmured Ben as the zookeeper picked his way back through the habitat, splashing up to his ankles in the artificial swamp.

"This isn't what we're about, boss," Klaus pleaded. "A few chipmunks to look cute for the kiddies. We had a good thing going."

The baby's short reptilian legs undulated slowly as Mr. Nastase stepped out of the exhibit with his prize. "That's small thinking from someone as big as you. Better animals mean higher prices and more tickets sold. Get some twine to tie the mouth shut. Now, where to next? I hear they've got a Komodo dragon. Or lemurs — they're all the rage since that movie. . . ."

As scared as he was, Griffin could not remain silent. "You'll never get away with this. Don't you think the cops will notice when your boat has exactly the same species that are missing from this place?"

The zookeeper nodded approvingly. "That's exactly why I'll have to throw open some of the cages. No one will notice a handful of absences in a mass escape. The police will allow for a few disappearances, the odd animal run over by a car —"

Klaus was alarmed. "A lot of them *will* get run over by cars!"

"Tragic," Mr. Nastase agreed. "But it's a sacrifice I'm willing to make."

"We'll rat you out," Griffin threatened.

"Who will believe you?" the zookeeper challenged. "A bunch of rotten kids in the middle of empty cages, zoo animals running wild — who do you think will get the blame?"

"That's not fair!" Ben blurted.

"Fair?" Mr. Nastase's mustache became positively alpine. "You break into my business, ruin my livelihood, make away with my valuable property, and leave my employee floundering in the ceiling like a man buried alive. And now you have the *nerve* to try to put my animals forever outside my reach. If you got what was *fair*, I'd throw you in with those alligators and lock the door. As it is, I'll enjoy following this in the news, watching you squirm. You'll have a lot of explaining to do, which is going to be hard" — without relaxing his grip on the baby alligator, he raised the tranquilizer pistol and pointed it at Griffin's chest — "considering you won't remember a thing."

Klaus regarded him with alarm. "Boss, no —!"

He jumped in front of the boys just as the zookeeper squeezed the trigger.

The sharp *pop!* was muffled outside the walls of the Reptile/Amphibian Center. But to Savannah, Pitch, and Logan, there was no question what the sound might be.

"A gunshot!" Logan rasped.

Savannah was horrified. "They're shooting the animals!"

"Never mind the animals!" Pitch hissed. "Griffin and Ben are in there!" She spoke urgently into the walkie-talkie. "Melissa — kill the lights."

At Base in Dr. Alford's office, Melissa had heard the shot via the walkie-talkie in Griffin's pocket. "What's going on?"

"*Now!*" Pitch insisted.

Melissa reached for the computer.

Griffin gaped at the tranquilizer dart that was now lodged in the fabric of Klaus's black jacket.

The security man seemed more confused than hurt. He regarded his employer in utter bewilderment. "Boss —?" Then he stumbled and collapsed to the floor at Griffin's feet.

Mr. Nastase's eyes blazed with anger, as if he couldn't believe his security man was lying down on the job. "You big oaf —"

And then everything went black.

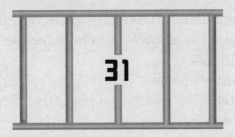

31

There was a gasp of shock from the zoo-keeper, followed by a skittering clunk that could only be the sound of a three-foot-long reptile hitting the terrazzo floor. With terrifying clarity, Griffin understood that the game had changed in a fundamental way. Even a baby alligator had a huge mouth filled with large, razor-sharp teeth. Desperately, he peered into the darkness. It was no use. He could make out nothing in the windowless corridor.

All at once, the door from the main hall was thrown open, and he was blinded by a flashlight beam. He squinted against the overpowering brightness, trying in vain to see behind it.

When he felt the tug, he cried out. But no, it was on his elbow — too high for the young gator to bite.

"Shhh — it's me."

"Pitch?" he whispered urgently. "What are you doing?"

"Rescuing you. Come on!" She grabbed his arm and hauled him out of the back corridor. Soon he was able to make out Savannah and Logan running beside them.

"Wait —" he began.

"No time!" They blasted through the double doors of the Reptile/Amphibian Center and into the cool night air.

Griffin was finally able to complete his sentence. "Where's Ben?"

Savannah and Logan exchanged accusing glances. "I thought *you* were getting Ben!" they chorused.

As one, they wheeled and headed back for the building. An earsplitting *blurp* cut the air, and an amplified voice commanded, *"Freeze!"*

Flashers blazing, a police cruiser swung up the zoo's main drive and screeched to a halt in front of the Reptile/Amphibian Center. Two uniformed officers leaped out.

Griffin took another step and was immediately skewered by the beam of a searchlight. "Don't try it!" came the harsh order.

But not even the long arm of the law could overrule Griffin's concern for Ben. "My friend's in there with two bad guys, and there's an alligator on the loose!"

That got the officers' attention. The cops barreled past them and pounded inside the building.

"The back hall!" Griffin instructed. He pulled the walkie-talkie from his pocket. "Melissa — turn the lights back on!" He was right behind the officers. Pitch, Savannah, and Logan brought up the rear.

The bulbs blazed — not the infrared of night mode, but bright fluorescent light.

An amazing sight met their eyes. Mr. Nastase was perched atop a work stool, treed there by the baby alligator, who was snapping at his heels. Not far away lay Klaus's titanic form, still unconscious from the tranquilizer dart. And curled against the opposite wall was Ben, relaxed and snoring softly, for all the world like he was in the comfort of his own bed.

The head cop was horrified. "Call animal

control and get me an ambulance! Possible alligator attack. I've got two people down — and one of them's a kid!"

"He's just sleeping," Griffin explained. "He does that a lot. As for the big guy, his boss tranqued him."

Mr. Nastase dropped the dart gun. "It was self defense! These are the kids who robbed my zoo! And they just attacked me with this dangerous predator!"

Savannah jumped forward and scooped up the baby alligator, gently holding its jaws shut. "That's a lie. And he's not dangerous. He's adorable."

Logan pointed at the zookeeper. "He's the one stealing animals."

The officer's eyes narrowed. "And what exactly are you kids doing here?"

"We're *giving* animals," Pitch put in defiantly. "We were on our way home when these guys ambushed us."

"In fact," Griffin added hopefully, "we should probably get going right now —"

"Don't even think about it. Nobody's at any of your houses. Your parents are all waiting for you at the police station."

The words resonated like cluster bombs. The zoobreak team had survived many near misses in the past week. But this was not going to be one of them.

Klaus sat up gingerly. "Oh, have I got a headache." As he blinked away the dizziness of the tranquilizer effect, his eyes focused on Logan. "Hey, isn't that Ferris Atwater, Jr.?"

Despite the trouble he knew they were in, Logan felt his heart swell with pride. Being recognized for a role you'd played was — a star sighting! His first ever!

Griffin bent down and shook Ben by the shoulder. "Wake up, man," he whispered. "We're under arrest."

32

It took a convoy of three police cars to gather up the zoobreak team and the staff of *All Aboard Animals* for the ride to the station. As if he wasn't miserable enough, the last thing Griffin saw before the cruiser left the grounds of the Long Island Zoo was the fleet of six Rollo-Bushels standing in the parking lot. Each prototype bore a large yellow tag that read EVIDENCE.

Griffin slumped in his seat beside Ben and Savannah. "I'm sorry, you guys. It's on me. I should have known that you can't keep piling plan on top of plan on top of plan without getting burned."

"No, this is my fault," Savannah said bravely. "It started with Cleo, and it mushroomed because I wouldn't leave all those animals on that hideous boat."

Ben was totally down. "Fine, you guys fight it out over who's guiltier. Just explain it to my mother before she kills me."

"My one consolation," Savannah added, "is that Klaus and Mr. Nasty are under arrest, too."

"Big deal," mumbled Ben. "We're in just as much trouble as they are. They stole animals; we stole animals. They broke in; we broke in. My luck, Klaus is going to be my cell mate in jail."

"I don't think Klaus knew anything about the stolen animals," Griffin put in. "He was trying to talk Mr. Nasty out of boosting the alligator. And that dart he took was meant for me."

"He's a saint," Savannah muttered sarcastically.

"What I don't understand," Griffin went on, "is how our parents found out where we were."

Ben was listless. "What difference does that make? So they knew in advance — big deal. When the cops caught us, they would have called our folks anyway. Same result — we're dog meat."

"Don't you see the difference?" Griffin reasoned. "Someone must have ratted us out. But who?"

When they arrived at the police station, the squad room was crowded, but the first face they saw was the guilty countenance of Darren Vader.

"I should have known," said Griffin through clenched teeth. "No situation is ever so bad that it can't get worse by Darren being involved."

But Darren seemed interested only in Mr. Nastase. "There he is! That's the guy who stole my owl and blackmailed me into telling on my friends!"

Pitch was annoyed. "Since when are we your friends?"

Griffin shushed her. Darren might be able to expose just the kind of man the zookeeper was. That was the only thing that could save them — the fact that everything they'd done had been to rescue the animals from Mr. Nastase's cruelty.

The sight of their children, alive and unhurt, was so welcome to the parents that there was a lot of relief and very little anger.

Griffin had an extra apology for his father. "Dad," he said, shamefaced, "I'm so sorry I got your prototypes impounded by the cops. I swear I wouldn't have done it if there was *any* other way to get all those animals to the zoo."

Mr. Bing sighed. "Let's hope it's just for a few hours. I wouldn't be so worried if the paperwork for the patent had been filed." He cast a resentful look in the direction of Darren's mother.

Griffin's mother spoke up. "Well, I say hurray for Daria Vader. She may not appreciate your newest invention, but at least she had the smarts to confront her son when she knew something was fishy. Who knows what would have happened if the police hadn't arrived when they did?"

Griffin nodded in reluctant agreement. Against all odds, Darren's big mouth might actually have done some good for a change.

"What I can't understand," Mom went on, "is why you always have to go off half-cocked on these crazy misadventures instead of just coming to *us*! We're your parents, not your enemies! Honestly, Griffin, if you were so dead set on rescuing those animals, why didn't you just *ask*?"

Griffin was chastened but unrepentant. "Think about it, Mom. Did you want me to ask you so you could *help*, or so you could talk me out of it?"

She sighed. "Maybe you have a point. But it's my responsibility to try to keep you from getting yourself killed, and that's what very well might have happened tonight."

It stung, mostly because she was right. Griffin had always believed that, with planning, kids could get along in the adult world. Yet the chaotic scene in the back hallway of the Reptile/Amphibian Center had him questioning himself. What would Mr. Nastase have done to them if Melissa hadn't killed the lights just in time? What if Klaus had gone along with his boss instead of stepping in front of the dart meant for Griffin? What if the baby alligator had bitten Ben in the dark? Griffin had to face the fact that there were situations that called for adult intervention, even if that meant the plan had to fail. Some things — like your safety and the safety of your friends — were more important than winning.

The buzz of whispered conversation turned to silence when Mr. Nastase and Klaus were paraded into an interrogation room. Both men were now in handcuffs.

Griffin rushed over to the officer who was bringing up the rear. "Don't be too hard on the big guy. He really came through for us in the end."

Mr. Bing held his son back gently but firmly. "Let's just let the police do their job."

That job was not a quick one. It was nearly three a.m. when Mr. Benson asked the desk sergeant if it might be better to take the kids home for a few hours' sleep and reconvene in the morning.

"Sit tight, sir," the officer replied gravely. "We're trying to get a handle on this whole situation."

The tone was echoed by all the cops at the precinct. The words were polite, even friendly. But their expressions were dead serious.

The arrestees remained with their parents, waiting in stiff-necked misery. There was no communication among the zoo-breakers themselves. Even Darren kept his mouth uncharacteristically shut. He wasn't in trouble with the law, but it was obvious that the Vaders were not happy with the role he had played in this caper.

Griffin caught Ben looking his way a few times, but Mrs. Slovak pointedly stepped in to block her son's line of sight. Not since the baseball card heist had Ben's mother regarded Griffin with such suspicion. She was probably thrilled that, nine days from now, Ben would be in New Jersey, away from the evil influence of The Man With The Plan.

Failure. Arrest. The Rollo-Bushels impounded. Ben headed for the DuPont Academy. There was so much to be sad about.

By four o'clock, Ben was fast asleep between his parents, and even Griffin was beginning to nod off, when the lieutenant himself came out to address the anxious families.

"I need everybody's attention —"

"Wait!" Savannah leaped to her feet. "*I'm* the only one who should be under arrest! *I* talked everybody into rescuing Cleopatra, and it was my idea to take the other animals, too! None of this would have happened if it wasn't for me!"

"Honey —" her father began.

"Let me finish!" She turned back to the lieutenant, her face impassioned. "You have to let the others off the hook! Whatever they did, it was because of me. And even if I have to go to jail for the rest of my life, you can't give those animals back to Mr. Nasty, because he is a cruel and terrible person. He doesn't understand them, he doesn't treat them right, and he definitely doesn't give them the love and respect that they deserve."

The lieutenant waited patiently through this long speech. "Are you done?"

Savannah sat down again, nodding bravely.

"Thanks. Well, what I came to say is this: Go home."

Mr. Kellerman looked cautiously optimistic. "And then what happens?"

The officer let out a heavy sigh. "Contrary to what you may think, a cop's job is more than eating doughnuts and yelling at teenagers to turn down the stereo. While you've been cooling your heels here, we've done some investigating. We know, for example, that there have been more than three hundred complaints about conditions at *All Aboard Animals* over the past eighteen months. We've also been in touch with the emergency staff that was called in to the Long Island Zoo tonight. They tell us that the 'extra' animals are all fine and in very good shape — and the places you stashed them showed care and a lot of thought. And after a heart-to-heart chat with your friend Mr. Nastase, our officers are on their way to make arrests in an exotic animal ring, responsible for stealing the Drysdale monkey and a certain meerkat that was reported missing from Barrington, Rhode Island, six months ago."

Parents and zoobreakers alike digested this information. When someone finally spoke, it was the shyest person in the group — and her timid voice barely made it past her curtain of hair.

"So . . . we're not under arrest anymore?" Melissa ventured.

"Only because there are people older and guiltier than you in this mess," the lieutenant said sternly. "Just because you did it for all the right reasons doesn't make it okay. Another thing that came up in our investigation was the little matter of a stolen Babe Ruth baseball card last fall. This is what we in the law enforcement community call a pattern. You lucked out on that one, too, but be warned: Your lucky streak is officially over. If your names come across our blotter again, it's going to go just like on the TV shows. You'll be arrested, cuffed, fingerprinted, and prosecuted to the full extent of the law. Now, I repeat — go home."

The collective sigh of relief moved the air in the room. Slowly, as if this break might be too good to be true, everyone stood and began to straggle toward the exit.

Savannah regarded her teammates. "I'm so sorry, you guys."

"Don't apologize," said Pitch stoutly. "We knew what we were getting into."

"I'm sorry, too," put in Darren. "I didn't want to mess you up. I mean, I wanted to mess you up, but — I would have been sad if any of you got eaten by an alligator."

From Darren Vader, that was heartfelt emotion.

When Mr. Dukakis opened the door, there was a whoop of merriment, and a young patrolman came wheeling into the squad room on an impounded Rollo-Bushel, executing spins and hairpin turns. Grinning like a kid at Six Flags, he jumped off in front of his commanding officer. "This thing is amazing, Lieutenant! Somebody ought to patent it!"

Mr. Bing's eyes locked with Mrs. Vader's across the group. She was, after all, the lawyer who was supposed to help him.

She nodded, impressed. "First thing Monday morning."

33

Dr. Kathleen Alford returned from her trip to Africa to find that the population of the Long Island Zoo had increased by more than just the three rain forest baboons she had brought with her. With the aid of her young friend Savannah Drysdale, she set to work finding new homes for the former *All Aboard Animals* collection.

She also hired a new assistant zookeeper — a burly young man with zoo experience, who would have no problem dealing with even the largest animals. Klaus Anthony had already been cleared in the case against his former boss, Mr. Nastase. His final act as an *All Aboard Animals* employee was to help the coast guard get the abandoned paddleboat out of the inlet at Rutherford Point. Once the engine had been coaxed back to life, a loud, grinding clatter cut the air. The giant paddlewheel made a single revolution before dumping several splintered, seaweed-tangled wooden planks onto the deck — the last remains of a discarded rowboat.

Mr. Nastase pleaded guilty to receiving stolen goods, attempted theft, and reckless discharge of a tranquilizer gun. In exchange for his testimony against the stolen-animal ring, he avoided jail time and was sentenced to fifteen hundred hours of community service for a wildlife preservation group. His job, though, would be in the mail room. He was banned from ever having direct contact with animals again.

Thanks to her extensive connections with zoos and preserves around the country, Dr. Alford had little trouble relocating her newest tenants. The meerkat went back to its owners in Rhode Island. The loon and the duck got the okay to return to the park next to Savannah's house. The loon in particular had become a neighborhood celebrity. The piglet and chicken, friends to the end, went together to the Queens County Farm Museum.

The squirrels and chipmunks were released into a wooded area. The hamsters, gerbils, mice, turtles, salamanders, and frogs were distributed to various pet stores. The beaver went all the way to a provincial park in Canada. The rangers there were amazed that it refused to cut down trees but instead built its dam by dismantling an old piece of furniture that had been dumped by the creek.

Darren's owl escaped while being trans-ferred to the Central Park Zoo and took shelter in the bell tower of St. Sebastian's Church on First Avenue, where it eventually made its home. Hoo was on First.

The chuckwalla was adopted by a large beach resort in Aruba to star in their TV commercials as Chuck Walla, Party Lizard. They guaranteed a climate-controlled home, celebrity status, and all the flies he could eat. His sauna days were just beginning.

The deal had been set to transfer the prai-rie dog and ferret to the San Diego Zoo. But when their female ermine gave birth to an oversized litter, it was no longer feasible to introduce a new male into the habitat. The prairie dog was still welcome; Ferret Face had to stay behind.

Dr. Alford's brow furrowed. Savannah would be upset. The poor girl felt guilty enough. To leave the ferret homeless would eat her alive.

And then the phone rang.

"How about these?"

Griffin tossed over another pair of pajamas, which Ben jammed into the suitcase.

"Why not?" he said listlessly. "It's a sleep academy. I might as well be dressed for it."

It was a moment both of them had been dreading. While Savannah, Melissa, Logan, Pitch, and even Darren had been basking in the relief of being off the hook for the zoo-breaks, he and Ben had been looking ahead to something far worse. The fateful day had finally come. Ben was departing for the DuPont Academy.

Griffin checked his watch. "I thought you guys were supposed to be leaving around noon. It's after two."

"My folks got a call for a last-minute conference with the pediatrician. The school nurse is there, too."

Griffin frowned. "That doesn't sound good."

Ben shrugged miserably. "I'm on my way to New Jersey. How much worse can things get?"

As if on cue, a car door slammed outside.

Ben took a deep breath. "This is it."

Griffin took an even deeper one and resolved not to make an idiot out of himself. *It's New Jersey, not the moon. . . .*

"Ow!!"

"My dad!" Ben exclaimed in alarm.

The two ran out of the room and started down the stairs to Mr. Slovak's aid.

An unidentified furry object came streaking toward them. It leaped on Ben, knocking him flat on his back on the first landing.

Ben gawked as the creature burrowed under his shirt and made itself comfortable.

"Ferret Face?!"

"Yeah, and he nearly bit off my finger!" Mr. Slovak complained. "In the future, keep him away from me."

"Future?" Ben echoed. "There *is* no future. I'm going away to school."

"Dr. Patterson and Nurse Savage noticed that your sleeping habits were improving," his father explained. "When they found out about Ferret Face, they got an idea and ran it by the experts at the academy. We give you back the ferret, and he keeps you awake during the day, which in turn makes you sleep better at night."

Ben was incredulous. "And DuPont agreed to that?"

Mr. Slovak nodded. "They're even sponsoring the trial. After six months, if this is working for you, then you won't have to go to the academy." He sucked on his finger. "And I repeat: Keep that monster away from me."

Ben hugged the ferret protectively. "He's not a monster; he's my personal guardian angel!"

His father grinned. "Good news, Ben. Better than good. Mom and I are thrilled."

The process of unpacking was much more joyful, and quicker, too. Ben ripped open his suitcase, dumped everything out on the floor, and set Ferret Face down to play in the soft clothing.

"All right, little buddy, go to town. You can even eat my socks. You're the man."

"It's amazing how things work out," Griffin observed. "This never could have happened without Operation Zoobreak."

"True," Ben told The Man With The Plan.

"But you have to admit that there are some times when even a perfect plan won't help you. You need a miracle."

"Like this," Griffin agreed.

What neither said aloud was that the greatest miracle of all was the fact that the two best friends on the planet were lucky enough to be growing up as neighbors in the very same town.

Down the street, in the Drysdales' yard, Cleopatra clung to the back of Luthor's neck — the second-best friends on the planet, blissfully happy to be together.

ABOUT THE AUTHOR

Gordon Korman's last novel featuring Griffin Bing and his team, *Swindle*, was called "pure plot-driven fun from top to bottom" by *School Library Journal* and "scary, funny, and hysterical" by a middle school reviewer in the *Chicago Tribune*. His other books include *This Can't Be Happening at Macdonald Hall* (published when he was fourteen); the trilogies Island, Everest, Dive, and Kidnapped; the series On the Run; and *No More Dead Dogs* and *Son of the Mob*. He lives in New York with his family and can be found on the Web at www.gordonkorman.com.

GRIFFIN BING HAS BEEN FRAMED!

When Griffin's new principal—Coach Lombardi—finds
Griffin's retainer in the school display case where a missing
Super Bowl ring should be, it's game over for Griffin. And
when Griffin's team fumbles its attempts to prove his
innocence, Griffin ends up in an alternative school, and then
under house arrest with an electronic anklet! Griffin smells
a rat—but will he be able to solve the mystery in time?

GO ON MORE THRILLING ADVENTURES WITH
GORDON KORMAN!

In this suspenseful series, teens fight for survival after being shipwrecked on a desert island.

Who will be the youngest person to climb Everest? Find out in this adventure-filled series!

In this action-packed trilogy, four young divers try to salvage sunken treasure without becoming shark bait!

Two kids become fugitives in order to clear their convicted parents' names in this heart-stopping series.

The hunt is on after Aiden's sister is abducted right before his eyes in this action-packed adventure trilogy.